THE BOY WHO SAVED CHRISTMAS

Vincent McDonnell

The Collins Press

Published in 2004 by
The Collins Press,
West Link Park,
Doughcloyne,
Wilton,
Cork

First published in 1992 by Poolbeg Press

© Vincent McDonnell 2004

Vincent McDonnell has asserted his moral right to be identified as author of this work.

British Library Cataloguing in Publication data.

ISBN: 1-903464-18-8

Printed in Malta

1
Mister Carbuncle

Mister Carbuncle was fat. He was like a giant football with a small head stuck on at one end, two short arms at his sides and two short legs at the other end. He was so fat he had to wriggle to get through a doorway. This usually made his face glow as red as a fire coal.

Mister Carbuncle was nasty. He was the nastiest man in the whole world. He liked nothing better than to see people suffer. He disliked everyone but detested children and animals above all.

Mister Carbuncle was a criminal and The Boss of The Underworld. Every criminal in The Underworld owed allegiance to him. Every robber and thief and burglar and mugger and thug was under his control. Each year they had to promise to serve him and to give him half of their ill-gotten gains.

Mister Carbuncle was very rich. In the house in which he

lived there was a secret room in the cellar. In it there was a great wooden chest with steel bands about it. It was filled to the brim with gold and jewels which sparkled in the light. Beside it was another chest. But this chest was only half filled with gold and jewels.

Mister Carbuncle was greedy. He wanted to have more and more gold and jewels. He wanted to fill the second chest and then a third and a fourth. He wanted to fill the room in the cellar with chests of gold and jewels.

For a year now the crooks of The Underworld had been working night and day. They robbed banks and post offices and jewellers' shops. They stole from rich men. They mugged old ladies and old men for their pensions. But still Mister Carbuncle's second chest remained half empty.

This upset Mister Carbuncle. He couldn't sleep at night. He tossed and turned in his great bed, thinking of how he might fill the chest. He went off his food. When he sat down to dinner he only ate two or three large helpings. And he only ate two dozen bowls of his favourite strawberry-flavoured ice-cream each day now.

He began to get thin. His enormous belly got smaller and smaller. It was as if the air was slowly going out of the giant football. One day he looked down and saw his toes . 'I'm wasting away,' he cried. 'I'm dying of hunger.' He was so frightened that he ordered extra large helpings for his lunch.

Afterwards he ate eighteen bowls of ice-cream. Then he ate four large sweet cakes.

Mister Carbuncle was satisfied for a few days. Then he began to worry about his riches again and lost his appetite once more. So he sent for his adviser, Mister Illegal, who was a lawyer. He too was a criminal who had stolen his clients' money and had been sent to prison.

In prison Mister Illegal met Mister Vicious who was Mister Carbuncle's right-hand man. Mister Vicious was as savage as a cornered wolf. He had fangs instead of teeth and drooled from the mouth. He had brought Mister Illegal to The Underworld where he had become Mister Carbuncle's adviser.

Mister Illegal was as thin as a telegraph pole and his shadow was like a black line drawn on the ground. His eyesight was poor because he spent years and years peering closely at documents, trying to figure out how to cheat his clients out of more and more money. Because of this he wore glasses with lenses so thick they looked like the bottoms of bottles. His face was as thin as the head of a hatchet and the black clothes he wore were shiny with age. His fingers were long and brittle like twigs.

Mister Illegal entered the room where Mister Carbuncle was trying to relax. The room was in darkness. Mister Carbuncle loved the darkness and all dark and evil things. Because of this he had the room painted black and there were

3

black blinds on the windows.

Mister Carbuncle was lying on a huge bed. It was a four-poster hung with black lace and silk. It had once belonged to a great prince but Mister Carbuncle's thugs had stolen it. It was the only bed in the world that would support Mister Carbuncle's vast weight without breaking.

There were rails attached to the side of the bed just like those on a baby's cot. Mister Chisel the carpenter had made the rails. They were fitted because Mister Carbuncle rolled about in his sleep. And because he was round like a football he used to roll out of the bed. One night he had rolled onto the floor and broke five of the floorboards. He had squashed his nose until it was as flat as the nose of a boxer. The next day he ordered his carpenter to make and fit the rails.

In the darkness Mister Illegal peered about trying to get his bearings. He stumbled towards the bed, his hands held out before him. He banged his knee against a chair and cried out in pain.

Mister Carbuncle laughed. He liked nothing better than to hear someone cry out in pain. It gave him great pleasure. Now his belly quivered and the bed shook. Then the room shook until it seemed like an earthquake was taking place.

Mister Illegal edged close to the bed. He felt the rails and held onto them. 'You sent for me, sir,' he said, addressing Mister Carbuncle as once he addressed his clients. Mister Illegal's voice quivered. He was terribly frightened of Mister Carbuncle.

'The second chest in the cellar is still half empty,' Mister Carbuncle said. 'I had expected to see it filled with gold and jewels by the end of the year. I want to know why it isn't filled.'

'Please, sir,' Mister Illegal said in a quavering voice. 'It is a very large chest. It will take years to fill it. You must be patient.'

'Patient!' Mister Carbuncle roared. 'Patient! Don't you realise that I'm wasting away with worry. I am eating only six meals a day. If this goes on much longer I will simply disappear. And you tell me to be patient!'

'Everyone is working so hard,' Mister Illegal said. 'They are working night and day. They are robbing more and more banks. They are stealing from everyone. They can't do any more, sir.'

'Can't do any more!' Mister Carbuncle yelled. 'How dare you say such a thing. I'm dying of hunger and worry. Don't you know that I ate only eight bowls of ice-cream so far today. It was my favourite ice-cream too – strawberry flavour with pints of lovely chocolate sauce poured over it.'

'I'm very sorry, sir,' Mister Illegal murmured.

'Sorry!' Mister Carbuncle roared like a lion. 'You're sorry! I'm giving you 24 hours to devise a plan to make me rich. To fill my chest in the cellar with gold and jewels. If you don't I'll … I'll …'

Mister Carbuncle's face became bloated with rage. His big nose was so red that it glowed in the dark like a lamp. 'I'll …' he repeated, trying desperately to think up a terrible punishment for Mister Illegal. 'If you don't come up with a plan in 24 hours,' Mister Carbuncle went on, triumphant at last, 'then I'll make you eat ice-cream.'

'Oh no! No!' Mister Illegal wrung his hands. He hated ice-cream. It was cold and sweet and it hurt his teeth. 'Not that,' he pleaded. 'Please don't make me eat ice-cream.'

'You've got 24 hours,' Mister Carbuncle warned. 'After that you're going to have to eat nothing else but ice-cream for the rest of your life. Now get out.'

'Thank you, sir,' Mister Illegal said. 'I promise to think of a scheme to fill the chest.' He bowed to Mister Carbuncle's huge mass, staring all the time at the gleaming red glow of his nose.

Mister Illegal backed towards the door, never once taking his eyes from the red glow. It reminded him of Rudolph the red-nosed reindeer. And it put an idea into Mister Illegal's mind as to how he might fill the chest. It was the right time of year too for his plan. There were only four weeks to Christmas.

It was a time of year Mister Illegal hated almost as much as he hated ice-cream. At Christmas everyone was happy. The laughing faces of children were to be seen everywhere. They depressed Mister Illegal and prevented him from thinking up his schemes.

6

But this year it would be different. Mister Illegal would want to see children happy. For every happy child would mean more gold and jewels for Mister Carbuncle. With the second chest filled to the brim Mister Carbuncle would be happy too. He would then forget that he'd ever threatened to make Mister Illegal eat ice-cream for the rest of his life.

Mister Illegal went back to his rooms. He summoned his chief clerk Mister Scribble and ordered him to bring him every book dealing with Christmas and Santa Claus. 'Immediately,' Mister Illegal ordered. 'I don't wish to be kept waiting.'

'Christmas?' Mister Scribble mumbled. 'Santa Claus? Why, I think Mister Illegal has finally gone off his head.' He got the necessary books and delivered them to Mister Illegal's room. There Mister Illegal spent all night poring over the books and making plans.

2
Christmas is Coming

It was cold at the North Pole. The wind howled across the vast white waste of the Arctic. The driven snow whirled about like falling leaves in the autumn. On the frozen ice-cap the baby polar bears snuggled closer to their mothers for warmth and comfort.

But in Toyland it was warm and snug. Huge log fires burned brightly in the grates. Now and then, showers of sparks burst from the burning logs like the stars in a fireworks display. But these weren't just any ordinary sparks. Like everything else in Toyland, they were magical. Wherever the sparks touched, the spot glittered and sparkled. It was like the dew on a spider's web caught in the morning sun. Everywhere clothes and furniture and all the toys glittered as if they were set with diamonds.

But Santa Claus and his elves hardly noticed the glitter. They were too busy. It was almost Christmas time and there was so much to do. Every year there were more and more children born in the world. The elves were kept busier and busier making extra toys so that no child should be without a present on Christmas morning.

Some of the elves were busy cutting and sewing. Others were sawing and hammering and planing and sanding. Still others were nailing and gluing and trying and testing. It was important that each toy worked well on Christmas morning. There were toy cars speeding about tooting their horns. Trains ran hither and thither, whistling and blowing off steam. Dolls were crying and laughing and walking and talking. Rocket ships flew up to the ceilings. Aeroplanes looped the loop while helicopters hovered just above the ground.

The noise was deafening. Any humans there would have to clap hands over their ears. But the man who now watched all of this activity didn't clap his hands over his ears. In fact he loved to hear the noise and watch the toys being made and tested.

He stood on a platform high in the air. From there he had a view of all of Toyland. He could see the elves at work. Around him on the thousands and thousands of shelves which reached from the floor to the ceiling were all the toys which had passed the test. They were now ready to be wrapped as presents.

There were nurses' uniforms and doctors' uniforms. There were suits for spacemen. There were games and puzzles and tricks. There were washing-machines and baking-sets. There were tools for carpenters and mechanics. There were sewing-machines and knitting-machines. There were things to make and things to eat. There was everything there that a child might wish for.

Just then one of the senior elves climbed onto the platform. He walked up to the watching man. 'Santa Claus,' he said. 'Rudolph and the sleigh are now ready. It's time you left on your journey.'

'Time to go already?' Santa Claus asked. 'It seems like only yesterday since I last met all the children in the world.' He looked around Toyland a little sadly. This was his home and the elves were his friends. He loved them all very much and disliked leaving them. But he loved the children of the world too. He enjoyed meeting them and sitting them on his knee. He liked to talk to them and listen to their stories. He liked to hear them tell him what they wished for at Christmas. He loved to promise them that he would do his best to bring them their special present. But best of all he loved to see the children sleeping on Christmas Eve when he called to all the houses in the world with a gift for every child.

'I'd best be off then, I suppose,' Santa said. He reached out a hand to the bell which hung beside him and pulled the cord.

It was a magic bell and its peals could be heard above the loudest noise. The elves stopped working. All the toys stopped too.

'My good friends the elves,' Santa Claus said, 'it is time for me to go and meet all the children in the world. I will find out what each child wants for Christmas. And no child will be disappointed. You have been busy throughout the year and all our shelves are packed with toys. I will tell all the children how hard you have worked.'

'Thank you, Santa Claus,' the elves called out.

'I will return on Christmas Eve,' Santa went on. 'By then you will have all the presents wrapped and ready. I will have a very busy night ahead of me so there will be no time to lose.'

'They will be ready,' the elves replied.

'Very good,' Santa Claus said. 'And now I must leave you.'

'Three cheers for Santa Claus,' the senior elf called out.

'Hip Hip Hooray! Hip Hip Hooray! Hip Hip Hooray!' At the last cheer all the elves took off their knitted caps and threw them up into the air. Santa Claus waved and sauntered off the platform. He followed his senior elf to the take-off ramp where Rudolph was hitched to the sleigh. Because only Santa Claus himself was travelling, only one reindeer was required to draw the sleigh. 'Hello, Rudolph,' Santa Claus said. 'Are you ready for our long journey?'

'Yes, Santa Claus,' Rudolph replied. 'Ready and waiting.'

'Then there's no time to waste,' Santa Claus said. 'The

11

children of the world are waiting for us.' With that he got up on the sleigh and sat in his well-padded, and comfortable seat.

'Goodbye, Santa Claus,' the senior elf said. 'We will see you again on Christmas Eve.'

'Goodbye,' Santa Claus called. He took up the reins in his gloved hands and shook them. Rudolph began to move forward. Quickly he gathered speed. He raced up the ramp, his breath like puffs of steam from a kettle. Faster and faster he went. At the top of the ramp Santa Claus gently pulled back on the reins.

Rudolph lifted his head and faced the stars. His hooves left the ramp and he climbed up into the sky. Santa Claus again tugged gently on the reins. Rudolph turned in the direction of the pull and headed upwards towards the moon.

'Easy now, Rudolph,' Santa Claus said. 'We have a long journey before us.' He looked downwards and saw the glitter of all of Toyland below him. 'Goodbye, my good friends,' he said. 'I'll see you soon.'

He would meet all the children of the world. But he was especially looking forward to seeing his special friend Timmy Goodfellow. The thought of meeting Timmy again took away his sadness. Santa took off his hat and waved it in the air. 'Ho! Ho! Ho!' he chuckled. Rudolph heard him and knew his master was happy. His heart leapt in his broad chest with delight and he quickened his pace. Swiftly the sleigh sped across the sky.

3
Timmy and Katie

Timmy Goodfellow couldn't sleep. He was much too excited because he was going to meet Santa Claus again tomorrow. Santa was paying his annual visit to Toys Galore. Next day Santa Claus would shake Timmy's hand and ask him how he and his little sister Katie were getting on. It would help ease the pain that Timmy and Katie felt since being orphaned.

Their father had been killed in an accident while Katie and her mother had both been badly injured. Katie's mother knew she would die, and in her hospital bed had called Timmy to her. She made him promise to take care of his sister. With tears in his eyes Timmy promised that he would do so.

Timmy and Katie had no other relations and they had to go and live with a woman called Mrs Haggard. She was tall and thin with a cruel face. She had long, grey, greasy hair which she never washed or combed. She never had a bath and she smelled awful. Her hands were long and scrawny and her fingers were white and knobbly. She had a nose like a witch. When she was angry, which was very often, her breath came out of her nostrils like small clouds of steam. She didn't like children. She thought they should be neither seen nor heard.

After the accident Katie couldn't walk and a judge gave her a large sum of money so she could pay for an operation to help make her walk again. Mrs Haggard knew this and wanted the money for herself. That was why she had taken Katie and Timmy. She promised to look after them but then found a doctor who was a criminal to sign a paper saying an operation would not help Katie. So Mrs Haggard was able to keep the money for herself.

Every day she made Timmy work hard. He had to clean and scrub and sweep and polish. Meanwhile Katie was left alone in her attic room. She cried because she was hungry and lonely. There was no fire so her little hands were always blue from the cold and the skin was chapped and blistered.

Mrs Haggard gave them little food. Mostly they had just bread and water. Now and again they got a tin mug filled with sour milk or some left-over potato. They were always hungry and it made Timmy sad to hear his sister crying.

'I'm so hungry,' Katie had sobbed one day just before

Christmas the year before. 'Please Timmy, could you get me some more food?'

Timmy dredged up his courage and went to see Mrs Haggard. 'Please, Mrs Haggard,' he said, 'we are very hungry. Could we have some more food please?'

'How dare you!' Mrs Haggard shouted. 'How dare you say you are hungry! You ... you're an ungrateful boy. To think I brought you and your sister into my home when you had no place else to go.' She spluttered. Steam came out of her nostrils as if she were a steam engine. She foamed and frothed at the mouth. Her long nose shivered and quivered. 'I'm going to punish you,' she added. 'You're a horrid boy.'

She caught Timmy by the ear and dragged him into the kitchen. It was a large, dark room with a huge fireplace. Mrs Haggard made Timmy sweep the chimney and collect all the soot in a bucket. She took the bucket and spilt the soot all over the tiled kitchen floor. Then she walked up and down and back and forward, trampling the soot with her heavy black boots. 'Now,' she said, 'I want you to clean the floor. I want it so shiny I can see my own reflection in it.'

Timmy stared at the floor in horror. It would take him hours and hours of scrubbing to clean it. With a heavy heart Timmy got the scrubbing brush. But Mrs Haggard took it from him and handed him a toothbrush instead. 'Use this,' she said. 'When you've finished you'll be sorry you upset me.'

'But …' Timmy gasped. 'Please, Mrs Haggard …'

'Quiet!' Mrs Haggard thundered. 'If there's another word out of you I'll bring your sister down here. She will have to go down on her knees to clean it. And for your insolence there will be no food for either of you tonight.'

Timmy didn't speak again. He hung his head as a sign of obedience to Mrs Haggard. Quietly he knelt down and began to scrub the floor. Hour by hour he scrubbed and washed and polished. When he had the floor shining he went to Mrs Haggard, who came and examined the floor. 'It's still not shiny enough,' she said. 'I want you to polish it some more.'

Inwardly Timmy groaned. But he couldn't refuse. He took up the toothbrush and began all over again. It was very late when he had finished. This time Mrs Haggard was satisfied. 'Let that be a lesson to you,' she said. 'Now get up to bed.'

Timmy and Katie slept in two cramped rooms in the attic. The windows were small and the rooms were always dark and murky. There was no ceiling and through the gaps between the slates, the stars and the moon could be seen in the sky. Katie and Timmy loved to look out through the gaps and see the glittering stars and the friendly man in the moon.

But when it rained, water dripped through the gaps onto the children sleeping in their beds. And when the wind blew through the gaps, it made the children shiver. So in the winter the rooms were as cold as a fridge. But in the summer when the sun shone, the slates got very hot and the rooms were like ovens.

As Timmy got to the top of the stairs he heard Katie crying. He crept into her room and over to the bed. It was bitterly cold in the room as it was now December. 'Don't cry, Katie,' he said. 'Timmy is here.'

'I'm hungry,' Katie wailed. 'Mrs Haggard never gave me any food.'

'It's my fault,' Timmy said. 'But you won't go hungry again I promise you. Tomorrow I'm going to get a job. I'll earn money and I'll buy you food and I'll save up so that you can have your operation. Then you'll be able to walk again and we'll both run away from here.'

'Thank you, Timmy,' Katie said. 'You're so good to me.'

'Sleep now,' Timmy said. 'While you're asleep you won't feel so hungry.' He sang a lullaby and soon Katie was sleeping. He tiptoed to his own room where he undressed and climbed into his cold bed. He was very hungry and he crouched in the bed holding his grumbling stomach in his hands.

The next day Timmy went out into the city. He passed Toys Galore and stopped to look in the window. In a corner of the window was a silver aeroplane with four great engines. Timmy would have loved to have had it for Christmas. In another part of the window was a doll in a pretty pink dress that Katie would love.

Timmy was about to turn away when he saw the sign. Boy Wanted, he read. Must Be Good Worker. Apply Mister Manager. Timmy was delighted and dashed into the store to see Mister Manager. He was shown into a large office where a tall, severe-looking man wearing a black suit sat behind a desk.

'You're a bit small, aren't you?' Mister Manager asked, when Timmy told him he'd come to apply for the job.

Timmy hung his head. He was very small for his age. But that was only because he'd had so little to eat. Then he thought of his younger sister and of the huge floor he'd cleaned last night. 'I'm a good worker, though,' he said. 'I'll work very hard.'

'Hmmm,' Mister Manager mused. He put his chin on his hands and pursed his lips. 'All right,' he said. 'I'll give you a chance.'

'Thank you,' Timmy said. 'Thank you. I will work hard, I promise.'

Timmy was as good as his word. He worked very, very hard. Each evening Mister Manager gave him money and Timmy bought food for himself and Katie. He had some money left over and he began to save it so that he could pay for Katie to have her operation.

One day the boy who demonstrated the computers was off sick. Mister Manager gave Timmy the job. Timmy was very bright and clever and all the parents and children liked him.

Mister Manager was very pleased. He told Timmy that he could work there from now on.

One morning, when Timmy arrived at the store, he found a large crowd of children waiting outside. Mister Mayor was there wearing his gold chain of office. All the important men from the city were there too. Mister Manager was hovering about like a rook in his black suit.

'What's happening?' Timmy asked another boy who worked in the store.

'You don't know?' The boy stared at Timmy in disbelief. 'Santa Claus is about to arrive,' the boy added. 'He always comes first to Toys Galore to meet the children.'

'Oh!' Timmy said. He would see Santa Claus. He wanted to run home and bring Katie here. But then he remembered she couldn't walk and that if he went away then he would lose his job.

Suddenly a shout went up from the crowd and children pointed up into the sky. Timmy followed their pointing fingers and saw Santa Claus' sleigh approaching. He was being drawn across the sky in his sleigh by Rudolph the red-nosed reindeer. They descended slowly and made a perfect landing, as if the sleigh was a light as a feather.

Mister Mayor and Mister Manager and the important men ran forward to greet Santa and shook his hand. Santa whispered something to Mister Manager and Mister Manager nodded. He in turn spoke to one of his assistants who ran to the sleigh and lifted into his arms what appeared to be a small bundle.

Santa Claus greeted the children and they waved flags and cheered. He shook children by the hand and asked how they were. As he entered the store he passed beside Timmy. Timmy's heart began to beat faster when Santa turned to him and held out his hand. Timmy couldn't believe it. He grabbed Santa's hand in his. 'How are you, my boy?' Santa asked.

'I … I … I …' Timmy couldn't speak. 'I …' he tried again. But the words stuck in his throat.

'This way. Make way, please. This way.' Mister Manager led Santa into the store. The crowd followed them while Timmy stood by the entrance in a daze. Santa Claus had shaken his hand! What a story he would have to tell Katie.

Just then the assistant passed by Timmy with the bundle in his arms. Timmy was surprised to see the bundle move. There was someone or something in there! The bundle moved again and a little face appeared. Two tiny eyes stared at Timmy. 'Where am I?' a little voice asked. 'Where's Santa Claus? I'm Elf Byte. I'm here to help Santa with his new computer.'

'It's all right,' the assistant said, and he passed into the store.

'An elf,' Timmy thought to himself. 'I've just met Santa Claus and a real elf. This must be the best day of my life.' He remained at the door still thinking of who he'd just met. Out of the corner of his eye he saw another assistant lead Rudolph away to feed him and give him water.

Timmy was still daydreaming when yet another assistant came running from the store. 'Timmy Goodfellow,' he said when he saw Timmy. 'You're to come to see Mister Manager immediately.'

Timmy's heart sank. In his excitement he'd completely forgotten his job. Now he would be sacked and he would earn no more money. Katie would never have her operation and they would both go hungry again.

With his heart almost breaking, Timmy hurried after the assistant. They both rushed through the store to Mister Manager's office. Timmy was trying to think of an excuse. But as he entered he stopped in surprise.

Mister Manager was sitting behind his large desk with a worried look on his face. Elf Byte was lying in a doll's cot. Santa Claus was standing beside the cot and he was stoking the elf's forehead.

'Ah, there you are, Timmy,' Mister Manager said. He turned to Santa Claus. 'Excuse me, Santa Claus,' he said, 'but here's that boy I was telling you about.'

Santa Claus swung about and looked at Timmy. 'You're Timmy Goodfellow,' he said. 'Mister Manager here tells me you're a genius with computers.'

'I ... I ... I ...' began Timmy.

'Speak up, boy,' Mister Manager said. 'Santa Claus is a busy man. He hasn't got all day to wait for you to speak, has he?'

'Yes, Mister Manager,' Timmy said. 'I … I mean no, Mister Manager. I mean …'

'Stop mumbling,' Mister Manager ordered. 'We have a serious problem. Santa Claus has introduced a computerised system to deal with the details of each boy's and girl's address and what they want for Christmas. Elf Byte here operates the system. Santa brought him with him for that purpose. But Elf Byte has never flown by sleigh before. He has got airsickness and is unable to work.'

'I'm fine now,' a little voice piped up from the cot. 'Honest I am.'

'You must rest today,' Santa Claus said. 'Then you'll be better tomorrow.'

'But the computer …' Elf Byte piped up.

'Timmy here will operate the computer,' Santa Claus said. 'Won't you, Timmy?'

'Me!' Timmy goggled. 'I …'

'Let's not have all that mumbling again,' Mister Manager said. 'Simply answer yes or no. Will you or will you not operate the computer?'

'I …' Timmy said. 'No. I mean … yes …'

'Great,' Santa Claus said. 'So let's get to work. We can't keep the boys and girls waiting. Come. We have no time to lose.'

Mister Manager led the way to Santa's Cave. They passed through the waiting crowd and the boys and girls stared at Timmy. 'Look, children,' a woman said, 'there's that wonderful boy who's going to help Santa Claus.'

Timmy felt he was six feet tall. He entered Santa's Cave and gazed about in wonder. He stared at Santa's chair and at the large sack of presents which lay at each side, one marked Boys and one marked Girls. Next to the chair was a table and on the table stood a computer.

Timmy sat at the table and switched on the computer. It was a special model made by some of the clever elves in Toyland. They had endowed it with magical properties. The computer could talk and it told Timmy what to do.

'Can you work it, Timmy?' Santa Claus asked.

'Yes, Santa Claus,' Timmy said. 'I can work it.'

'Very good,' Santa Claus said, taking his seat. 'Now send in the first child.'

All that day Timmy worked beside Santa Claus. As each boy and girl came into Santa's Cave Timmy entered their name and details of what they wanted for Christmas in the computer. He was very proud to help Santa and couldn't believe his good fortune. Some children were in awe of Santa and would only whisper. 'Speak up,' Santa would tell them. 'otherwise my friend Timmy won't hear you. Wouldn't it be terrible now if we brought you the wrong present?'

23

At those times Timmy had been especially proud. There was Santa Claus, who was the most important man in the world, calling little Timmy Goodfellow his friend.

At the end of the day Timmy was very tired. 'You've been a great help to me,' Santa Claus said. 'I couldn't have managed without you. Now enter your own name in the computer and also what you want for Christmas. Do you have any sisters or brothers?'

Timmy told Santa about Katie. 'Put her name in too,' Santa said. 'And tell me what she'd like.'

Timmy could hardly believe his luck. He entered both his own name and Katie's. He asked Santa to bring him the aeroplane and to bring Katie the doll with the pink dress. Santa promised that he would do so. 'And now,' he said to Mister Manager, 'give this boy a bonus. And when I call again next year I want Timmy to help me again with my computer.'

'Certainly, Santa Claus,' Mister Manager said.

Timmy could hardly believe it. He had helped Santa Claus. And he had got a bonus too. He and Katie would get presents for Christmas. And next year he would get to help Santa Claus again.

That evening Timmy waited outside the store until Santa Claus left. At the door Santa shook hands with Timmy and thanked him again for his help. 'Thank you too, Timmy,' Elf Byte piped up. 'You've done a wonderful job.'

Timmy's face glowed until it was as red as Rudolph's nose. He waited while the sleigh was brought round and Santa and Elf Byte climbed aboard. 'Goodbye, Timmy,' Santa said. 'I'll see you again next year.'

That evening as Timmy hurried home with lots of extra food and a wonderful story for Katie, next year seemed ages away. But Christmas came and when Timmy and Katie awoke on Christmas morning there were their presents by their beds. Then the New Year came and soon it was springtime. Summer burst upon them in a blaze of sunshine. The months passed and autumn crept near. The days grew shorter and the weather became colder. But Timmy didn't mind the cold weather. It told him that Christmas would soon come. And when it drew near Santa Claus would come again from Toyland.

Timmy and Katie counted the days. They drew a calendar on the wall and marked off the days one by one. There were twenty days to go, then ten days and five days. Four days, three, two, one.

The magic day was tomorrow. Tomorrow Timmy would go to Toys Galore. He would watch Santa Claus arrive in the sleigh. Santa would shake his hand and Timmy would go to Santa's Cave. He would be Santa's helper again as Santa had promised. And Santa Claus never broke a promise. It was the one thought in Timmy's head as he fell asleep at last and dreamt he was an elf in Toyland.

4
The Master Plan

Mister Carbuncle and Mister Vicious sat in the operations room at The Thieves' Den. This was the room where robberies were planned. There were maps hung on the walls with banks and post offices and jewellers' shops marked in red ink. In a corner of the room there was a television and video recorder. Here Mister Carbuncle showed videos of robberies so that he could train new thugs.

Mister Carbuncle and Mister Vicious were waiting for Mister Illegal to arrive. He had informed them that he had thought up a brilliant plan for obtaining more gold and jewels to fill Mr Carbuncle's wooden chests.

Mister Carbuncle and Mister Vicious were both drinking large glasses of whiskey and smoking fat cigars. 'What's keeping him?' Mister Carbuncle growled. He was an impatient man and hated to be kept waiting especially when the matter of more gold was to be discussed.

Mister Illegal eventually arrived. He was dressed in his black suit. He wore a white shirt and a black bowtie. He carried a black briefcase and looked like a rook who was turning into a lawyer. Or else a lawyer who was turning into a rook. 'Good day, gentlemen,' he began. 'I've summoned you both to this most significant conference for the singular reason of …'

'Cut the cackle,' Mister Vicious growled. 'Let's just hear your plan.'

'Yes, yes.' Mister Carbuncle sat upright in his chair. His little eyes were bright with greed.

'Very well.' Mister Illegal was upset. He loved the sound of his own lawyer's voice and liked to use big words to impress people. Now he turned about and switched on the television and the video. He took a tape from his briefcase, inserted it in the video and pressed the button marked Play.

Mister Carbuncle and Mister Vicious stared at the television screen. It showed a large store in the city. They weren't very good at reading and with difficulty spelled out the words Toys Galore. Outside the shop a large crowd of children were gathered. 'What is this nonsense?' Mister Carbuncle roared. He disliked children. Even the sight of children on the television screen gave him indigestion.

'Children?' Mister Vicious roared. He too was angry.

Whenever Mister Carbuncle got indigestion he made sure that his right-hand man also suffered. 'Don't you know that Mister Carbuncle dislikes children? You're not suggesting that we rob children of their pocket money?'

'What a good idea.' Mister Carbuncle removed his cigar and sat forward in his seat. 'It delights me to see children unhappy, Mister Vicious,' he added turning to his right-hand man. 'Let's put Mister Illegal's idea into action immediately.'

'Please.' Mister Illegal held up his hand. 'Most children receive on average a euro or two remuneration per week. Now currency of said magnitude would hardly constitute sufficient reason for us to contemplate instigating action for its removal thereof from such persons …'

'What's the idiot gabbling about?' Mister Carbuncle roared.

'He says robbing children of their pocket money wouldn't be worth our while,' Mister Vicious explained.

'Why bring up that idea then?' snarled Mister Carbuncle viciously. 'Are you trying to make a fool of me?'

'No, sir!' Mister Illegal was frightened. He was too frightened to even suggest that the idea had not been his. 'My proposition,' he mumbled, 'is different.'

'Well let's hear it then,' Mister Carbuncle roared. 'We haven't got all day to listen to you suggest ideas which you then say are no good. Now out with it. And in plain language. Otherwise I'll have your tongue cut out.' He stuck the cigar back in his mouth and began to chew the end.

'Pertaining to my proposition,' Mister Illegal began and then thought of the threat to his tongue. 'As you may be aware, gentlemen,' he continued, using small simple words and licking his lips with the self-same tongue, 'it will soon be Christmas.'

Mister Carbuncle groaned. If there was anything Mister Carbuncle disliked as much as children, it was Christmas. It was a horrible time with adults feeling happy and with smiling children everywhere.

Mister Illegal noticed that once again he had upset Mister Carbuncle and hurried on. 'Now at this time of year,' he added, 'all the parents in the world take their children to meet Santa Claus.'

Mister Carbuncle bit the end off his cigar. He stuttered and spluttered and Mister Vicious clapped him on the back. Mister Carbuncle spat out the end of his cigar. He grabbed his glass of whiskey and gulped it down. If there was one thing in the whole world Mister Carbuncle disliked more than children or Christmas, it was Santa Claus.

Mister Carbuncle began to growl like a mad dog. Quickly Mister Illegal went on. But not before he put his fingers to his lips and felt his tongue. 'The children tell Santa Claus what they want him to bring them for Christmas,' Mister Illegal said.

At this Mister Carbuncle cried out. He moaned and groaned. Never before had anyone said all of those horrid words in one sentence. Children, and Christmas and Santa Claus! Mister Carbuncle felt it was the worst moment of his life.

Mister Vicious poured him another whiskey and Mister Carbuncle gulped it down. Then Mister Vicious removed from his belt a long, wicked-looking knife. He felt the sharp edge with his thumb and licked his lips. It was perfect for tongue-cutting!

Mister Illegal nearly fainted. But somehow he managed to hurry on with what he was saying, not stopping to even draw breath. 'Children want lots of presents for Christmas,' he said. 'And presents cost lots of money. The parents give this money to Santa Claus to pay for all the presents'

'Money! Did he say money?' Mister Carbuncle recovered. He stared at his cigar and raised it to his mouth. Mister Vicious caught his hand just in time. In his excitement Mister Carbuncle had been about to put the lighted end between his lips.

'Substantial amounts of currency,' Mister Illegal said. 'If you would just momentarily peruse the television screen.' In his own excitement he'd forgotten again to use simple words.

But Mister Carbuncle or Mister Vicious didn't notice. Instead they looked at the screen. They could see Santa Claus sitting on his chair in Santa's Cave. He had a small boy on his knee. The boy was giving Santa a long list of all the presents he wanted for Christmas. Next to Santa sat another small boy who was entering all the details into a computer.

'The cost of the presents for that one boy comes to 154.73,' Mister Illegal said, remembering his tongue just in time. 'Now there are millions and millions and millions of children in the world. Every single one of them gets presents for Christmas.'

'A million times 154.73,' Mister Carbuncle said. He tried to work out the sum in his head but there were far too many noughts. At the thought of the noughts his eyes spun around. Round and round they went, faster and faster. Mister Carbuncle hated anything that turned or spun. It gave him a headache and made him ill. His face went green just as if he were seasick.

'I have the figures here,' Mister Illegal said. 'We are talking about not just one chest of gold and jewels, but many many chests.'

'Many many chests!' Mister Carbuncle recovered. There were no noughts on many many chests and his eyes no longer spun. 'Will there be enough chests to fill the room in my cellar?'

'Oh, undoubtedly,' Mister Illegal said. It was a phrase he used when he wasn't sure.

'So we rob Santa Claus of all this money?' Mister Carbuncle said. 'That should be easy. We'll have great sport.'

'It won't be easy,' Mister Illegal stammered. 'You see Santa

Claus won't have all the money at one time.'

'What?' Mister Carbuncle roared. 'You mean you've been making a fool of me again. Haven't I just told you no one makes a fool of me.'

'Please, sir. No!' Mister Illegal stammered. 'We don't rob Santa Claus.'

'Don't rob him!' Mister Vicious said. 'But you just said now that we would have some sport.'

'I didn't say ...' Mister Illegal began.

'Are you calling me a liar?' Mister Vicious again tested the edge of his knife on his thumb.

'No, my lord,' Mister Illegal said. In his fear he thought he was in a court of law. 'I mean, no sir, Mister Vicious, sir.'

'That's better,' Mister Vicious said. He preened himself like a turkey cock. He was especially proud when people called him sir.

'What I was going to suggest,' said Mister Illegal, hurrying on, 'is that we kidnap Santa Claus. Then we dress someone up in Santa's clothes and send him to meet the children. The parents will give the money to the mock Santa Claus who will give it to us.'

'You mean to me,' Mister Carbuncle said.

'I mean you, Mister Carbuncle.' Mister Illegal wrung his hands.

'And,' Mister Carbuncle said, 'who's going to pretend to '

be Santa Claus?'

'He will need to be fat,' Mister Illegal said. 'I thought yourself …'

'Are you suggesting that I'm fat?' Mister Carbuncle raged.

'No sir,' Mister Illegal said. 'But the person who pretends to be Santa Claus will need to resemble him.'

'It's out of the question,' Mister Carbuncle roared. 'I hate children. I couldn't bear to have them sit on my knee. They would have sticky fingers from eating lollipops and I would have to make them promise to be good. I'd hate that.'

'Think of all the lovely chests of gold and jewels,' Mister Vicious said. He didn't really care about the chests. But he didn't want Mister Carbuncle to get indigestion.

'All those chests,' Mister Carbuncle said slowly. 'My cellar filled with chests … I suppose I could put up with it. But I'll have to have all the gold and jewels for myself. It was my idea and if I'm going to have to pretend to be …' He couldn't bear to speak the name of Santa Claus again.

'Certainly, sir,' Mister Illegal fawned. 'It was your idea. And a first-class idea if I may so, sir.'

'Oh, shut up,' Mister Carbuncle shouted. 'Now tell us about my brilliant plan.' Mister Carbuncle grabbed his glass of whiskey and lit another cigar. Then he sat and listened to Mister Illegal's plan to kidnap Santa Claus, pretending all the time that the plan was his own.

33

5
Santa Sets Out

S anta Claus crossed the vast white expanse of the North Pole. Below he could see the ice glittering and glistening in the moonlight. In places there were great chunks of ice, some as big as the largest building in the world. Elsewhere the ice stretched flat for miles and miles like huge linen sheets spread out on the ground to dry.

It was very cold but Santa Claus was snug and warm. His red suit and coat had been made by the elves and possessed magical qualities which kept out the bitter Arctic cold. He wore three pairs of woollen socks. The elves had spun and then knitted the socks for him. They had endowed the wool with magical qualities and Santa's feet were cosy and warm in his black boots. His hat too had been made by the elves and this too kept Santa warm. His face was covered with his thick white beard. Only his nose was exposed and it now was red. But not as red as Rudolph's.

This was the time of year Santa Claus looked forward to most. He loved to come from his home in Toyland to meet all the children in the world. It gave him great pleasure to tell them he would bring them whatever they wanted on Christmas Eve. But this year Santa Claus was particularly looking forward to coming to Toys Galore. For soon he would meet Timmy Goodfellow again. Santa Claus was very impressed with Timmy. Though Timmy had never worked Santa's special computer before he hadn't made a single mistake.

This year Santa Claus hadn't brought Elf Byte with him. Elf Byte was delighted at this. Because no matter how much he practiced all through the year, he still suffered from airsickness. He still became ill at just the thought of going up in the sleigh.

Instead Santa Claus had decided he would ask Timmy Goodfellow to travel all over the world with him and work the computer. Santa Claus knew Timmy would be delighted. And so Santa was especially looking forward to meeting Timmy again and seeing the surprise on his face. Santa Claus liked nothing better than giving children surprises.

He chuckled to himself and pulled gently on the reins. Rudolph put his nose down and they began to descend. Lower and lower they flew. They skimmed above the ground, seeing the trees and fields and hedgerows and houses flash by. On they sped towards the city and the waiting children. On they sped towards Timmy Goodfellow. On they sped towards where Mister Carbuncle and his thugs were planning to kidnap Santa Claus.

That morning Timmy Goodfellow awoke at dawn. Immediately he leapt from his bed and dashed to the window. In the night Jack Frost had been at work. He'd drawn a magic tracery of ferns and leaves on the glass. But this morning Timmy had more important things to look for. He blew his breath on the glass. Slowly the frost melted and he looked out on the sleeping world. Only the birds were awake and they flew down onto the window-sill to pick from Timmy's hand the titbits he always kept for them.

'Have you seen Santa Claus and his sleigh yet?' Timmy asked.

'No, Timmy,' said Robbey Robin and Chirpy Sparrow.

'Neither sight nor sound of him, Timmy,' said Beaky Blackbird. Chalky Crow didn't say anything. He just shook his beak.

'Oh well, he'll be soon here,' Timmy said. 'I'd better get dressed.' He bade the birds goodbye and dressed quickly. Then he crept downstairs and listened at the door to Mrs Haggard's bedroom. He could hear her snoring and knew she had been out late the previous night enjoying herself and spending Katie's money. Still, it meant that she wouldn't be awake for ages yet. So it gave him the opportunity to prepare a nice breakfast for himself and Katie.

'Is it morning already?' Katie asked when he brought her breakfast.

'Bright and early,' Timmy said cheerfully.

'Today's the day, isn't it?' Katie asked.

Timmy nodded eagerly. 'I can hardly wait,' he said. 'Can you believe it's a whole year since I last met Santa Claus?'

'I'd love to meet him too,' Katie said.

'I'll ask him if he'll come and meet you,' Timmy said. 'But he's such a busy man ... And I promise to ask him to bring you a new dress for the doll you got last year. And the doll's pram you want.'

'Thanks, Timmy,' Katie said. 'You're the best brother any sister ever had.'

'I'm all right, I suppose,' Timmy said. He was shy and was embarrassed by the lavish praise. He stole a glance at his sister. She looked so much better now than she had looked last Christmas. Her cheeks were rosy and her long blonde hair shone. Her eyes sparkled again and she looked happy.

Thanks to Santa Claus Timmy still worked at Toys Galore. He earned lots of money to buy food and clothes for Katie and himself. He had a large sum saved for Katie's operation. They didn't want for anything except a mother's love and affection.

But there was little Timmy could do about that. The authorities said Mrs Haggard was their mother now.

When Katie finished her breakfast Timmy washed the cups and saucers and plates and put them away. Then he put on his anorak with the fleece lining and said goodbye to Katie. He crept downstairs and out of the house. It was very cold but Timmy hardly noticed. He was snug in his warm anorak and the brisk walking pace he set helped to keep him warm too. He headed in the direction of Toys Galore. Today was a very special day and he wanted to be there early to savour all the atmosphere.

Mister Carbuncle and Mister Vicious and Mister Illegal sat long into the night discussing their plan to kidnap Santa Claus. Mister Vicious had sent messengers out into The Underworld to recruit a number of thugs they would need to help them.

It was dawn before the thugs arrived. Each one looked as mean and vicious as the other. They had white pasty faces from having spent their lives in The Underworld or in prison. They had cruel eyes and stubble on their chins and stared suspiciously at everyone and everything. They all wore knuckle-dusters and bore the scars of many fights.

Mister Vicious gave them beer to drink and they sat

around talking among themselves about the fights they'd had and the time they spent in prison.

In another room Mister Sparks, who was a genius with electronic gadgets, sat hunched over a large radio. It had flashing lights and dials and knobs. Mister Sparks kept twirling one particular knob and listening intently on his headphones. Beside him Mister Carbuncle waited. He was eating a large bowl of ice-cream.

Mister Sparks twirled the dial a little more. 'Air Traffic Control to Santa Claus,' Mister Sparks spoke into a microphone. 'Air Traffic Control to Santa Claus. Can you read me? Over.'

The radio crackled. Then they all heard a voice come over loud and clear. 'Santa Claus to Air Traffic Control. Receiving you. Over.'

Mister Sparks held up a thumb to Mister Carbuncle. 'Air Traffic Control to Santa Claus,' Mister Sparks said. 'I wish to inform you of regulations banning flying over the city. Over.'

'Regulations,' Santa Claus repeated. 'What regulations? Over.'

'It only became law last night,' Mister Sparks said. 'If you wish to fly over the city you must do so in one of the new city helicopters. Do you understand? Over.'

'Understood,' Santa Claus said. 'But I have to be at Toys Galore to meet all the boys and girls. How can I get there on time if I don't fly there in my sleigh? Over.'

'There is a helicopter standing by to fly you to Toys Galore,' Mister Sparks said. 'If you land at the old airfield west of the city we will meet you there in twenty minutes. Is that understood? Over.'

'Message understood,' Santa Claus said. 'I'm turning for the west of the city now. Over and out.'

Mister Sparks flicked a knob on his radio. 'We've got him,' he said to Mister Carbuncle. 'We've got him!'

Mister Carbuncle made a grimace which was supposed to be a smile. 'He's taken the bait,' he shouted. 'Let's catch him while we can.'

Mister Carbuncle gulped down the ice-cream which dribbled down his chin. Then he led the way outside to where a helicopter waited. He climbed into the helicopter with his thugs and with a roar it took off. As it swept over the city a boy gazed up at it. He watched the helicopter until it was out of sight. Only then did Timmy Goodfellow enter Toys Galore.

6
Kidnapped

Santa Claus saw the great city slowly take shape before his eyes. The sun glistened on slate and sparkled on glass. He was always delighted to see it again. He knew that down there in the houses there were thousands of children. They would all be excited and getting ready to come and meet him at Toys Galore.

In one of those houses Timmy Goodfellow lived with his sister Katie. Santa Claus was looking forward to meeting them both. In fact he had two surprises for Timmy. When Santa had seen all the boys and girls at Toys Galore, he was going to take Timmy into the sleigh with him. They would soar over the rooftops and land on the roof of the house where Timmy and Katie lived. Santa Claus would shoot down the chimney with a whoosh and into the room where Katie was. What a surprise that would be for her!

He had almost reached the city. Soon he would be bringing his sleigh in to land on the concrete apron before Toys Galore. But Santa remembered the man from Air Traffic Control. Flying was now forbidden over the city. Santa Claus was a law-abiding person. He would never dream of breaking any rules or regulations.

He flapped on the reins and Rudolph immediately responded. He swung away from the sun and headed towards the west of the city. They flew over the fields where cows and a bull grazed the thin winter grass. As the shadow of the reindeer and sleigh passed over the land the animals looked up into the sky. Santa Claus waved to them and Rudolph nodded with his fine strong head.

The sleigh sped on. Soon Santa Claus saw the tumble down buildings of the old airfield. He tugged gently on the reins. Rudolph slackened his speed and began to descend. Down, down they drifted as gently as a snowflake. As they approached the ground Santa Claus could see the helicopter waiting before the great old aircraft hanger. There were two people waiting for him and his heart lifted. He would soon be at Toys Galore now.

The sleigh came in for a perfect landing. As it touched down Mister Illegal stepped forward. 'Good morning, Mister Claus,' he said. 'I'm Mister Illegal. I represent the city council,' he lied. 'I have here in my briefcase the necessary documents which you must sign before you can travel in the helicopter.'

'Documents?' Santa Claus asked. 'Can't they wait? I'm very late and the boys and girls at Toys Galore are waiting for me. I should have been there fifteen minutes ago.'

'I'm afraid they have to be signed now,' Mister Illegal said. 'It won't take a minute, I assure you. If you follow me. This gentleman here will take care of the reindeer and the sleigh.'

The thug referred to grinned at Santa Claus. Well it was meant to be a grin but was more like a grimace of pain. The edges of the man's mouth turned downwards and his top lip curled up until it touched his bulbous nose. He had only three teeth in his top gums. The one in the centre pointed down at his chin while the other two pointed towards each of his ears.

Santa Claus was worried. It didn't seem right. He was about to question Mister Illegal further but then remembered the boys and girls waiting for him. 'I'll sign the papers then,' Santa Claus said. 'But let's hurry. I have no time to waste.'

Mister Illegal led the way across to the hanger's huge entrance. As they approached Santa saw it was very dark inside. He hesitated but Mister Illegal beckoned to him to hurry. He followed Mister Illegal into the hanger and as he walked into the darkness two thugs stepped from the shadows and pinioned his arms.

A powerful light was switched on and Santa Claus saw standing before him the dreaded figure of Mister Carbuncle. Beside him stood Mister Vicious and another evil-looking thug. 'What's this?' Santa Claus demanded. 'I'm much too busy to be playing games.'

'It's not a game,' Mister Carbuncle said. 'We're making you redundant.'

'Redundant!' Santa Claus exclaimed. 'Don't be ridiculous! Santa Claus can't be made redundant.'

'We're giving you a rest then,' Mister Carbuncle laughed. All the other thugs laughed too. They didn't think it was funny but when Mister Carbuncle cracked what he thought was a good joke it was best if everyone laughed.

'But there'll be no Santa Claus then.' Santa was distraught. 'What will all the children of the world think?'

'Oh, but there will be a Santa Claus,' Mister Carbuncle said.

'Who?' Santa Claus demanded.

'Me!' Mister Carbuncle said. 'I'll be Santa Claus. Then the parents of all the children in the world will give me money. I'll be the richest man in the world. I'll have chests and chests filled with gold and jewels.'

'But the toys,' Santa Claus said. 'I buy materials to make toys with the money the parents give to me. If you keep the money for yourself then the children of the world won't have any toys.'

'They'll all be unhappy,' Mister Carbuncle chortled with glee. 'In fact everyone in the whole world will be unhappy on Christmas morning except me. I'll be counting my gold and I'll be very happy.'

'You villain!' Santa Claus said. 'You rogue!' He struggled to get free but the men who held his arms were enormously strong. Santa Claus only made himself breathless and red in the face.

'You can't do anything,' Mister Carbuncle laughed. 'You'll never be able to do anything again. From now on everyone in the world will think you're a thief. No one will ever like you again. No one will speak your name again. There'll be no Christmas any more.'

'Oh no!' Santa Claus exclaimed. A tear came into each of Santa's bright blue eyes. The tears tumbled from the corners of his eyes and ran down the deep furrows in his face. Tear after tear ran down until his lovely soft white beard was soaking wet.

Mister Carbuncle and his thugs laughed and laughed. They were cruel and heartless men and they liked nothing better than to see someone sad. They laughed until tears streamed down their faces too.

'Enough,' Mister Carbuncle roared. 'Take off Santa's suit and bring it to me immediately.' He strode off towards a small room which had once been an office. Mister Vicious and his thugs began to remove Santa's suit.

Mister Vicious brought Santa's suit to Mister Carbuncle. He looked at the bright red trousers, coat and hat. 'I can't put those clothes on,' he wailed. 'They're too bright. I only like to wear black.'

'No one else can pretend to be Santa Claus,' Mister Vicious said.

'Why not?' demanded Mister Carbuncle.

'Because you're fat,' Mister Vicious said.

'Fat! Did you say fat?' Mister Carbuncle hated anyone to say that he was fat. He grabbed Mister Vicious by the throat and shook him. 'Fat,' he roared. 'How dare you say I'm fat.'

'Plum … plum … plump,' Mister Vicious managed to say as his throat was squeezed tighter and tighter. 'I meant to say that you're plump.'

'That's better,' Mister Carbuncle said. He grabbed Santa's clothes and looked at them with distaste. But as he stared he saw chests of gold before his eyes. His greed made up his mind for him. Quickly he began to take off his own black clothes. He put on Santa's red trousers but his belly was much too fat and the trousers wouldn't fit him. 'They're too small,' he wailed. 'They won't fit me.'

'Give them to me,' Mister Vicious said. He took the trousers and examined them. 'There are generous seams,' he said. 'I think I will be able to do something with them.'

He took out his knife with the long blade and the edge like a razor. He slit the seam at the seat of the trousers and pinned it back together with safety pins. Mister Carbuncle put on the trousers and now, once he held in his belly, they fitted him.

Santa's coat and hat were also too small. But somehow, with the help of Mister Vicious, they eventually fitted. But Santa's boots wouldn't go on Mister Carbuncle and he had to leave on his own leather boots with the steel toe caps. 'I could have some fun with these,' he said. 'A sharp kick on the shin with those steel caps would really hurt a boy or girl.'

At this they both laughed. They liked to inflict pain and see people suffer. 'We're ready,' Mister Vicious said and they all trooped out to the waiting helicopter. Soon they were airborne and heading for Toys Galore.

Two thugs remained behind at the hanger. They threw Santa Claus in a dark corner and tied his hands and feet with strong ropes. He struggled but the ropes only got tighter. He was completely helpless. He would never escape. Then the thugs bound Rudolph's feet with strong ropes until he was as helpless as Santa Claus.

Then the two thugs stood on guard outside the hanger. They were two of the most vicious and cruel of all the thugs in the whole of The Underworld. Santa Claus and Rudolph would never be rescued while they were on guard.

7
A Very Different Santa

Timmy Goodfellow scanned the sky, hoping for a sight of Santa's sleigh. But the blue canopy with its feathery clouds belonged to the birds. Timmy was worried. Santa Claus was very late. But Timmy was not as worried as Mister Manager. Santa Claus had never been late before. 'I hope nothing's happened to him,' he whispered. 'He is an old man, after all.'

Timmy's heart pounded. Surely nothing could happen to Santa Claus? He anxiously looked into the sky again. But there was still no sign of Santa Claus or his sleigh.

Mister Mayor and the waiting dignitaries were growing impatient. They didn't like to be kept waiting. They had delicious lunches waiting for them at the Town Hall. They were all greedily thinking of their huge helpings and sipping steaming glasses of spiced punch.

Mister Mayor stamped his feet to keep them warm. Each time he moved, his heavy gold chain of office jangled. It irritated everyone but they were too frightened to say anything. Mister Mayor was the most powerful man in the city. Nobody wanted to offend him.

Suddenly Timmy Goodfellow heard a rackety clackety noise in the sky. Everyone else heard it too. Hundreds of heads swivelled in the direction the noise came from. Hundreds of eyes stared up into the sky.

Timmy saw the helicopter as it came over the roof of the Town Hall. It looked like a great black bird against the blue sky. Slowly it came nearer dropping down and down. The noise became deafeningly loud and Timmy could feel the wind from the rotor blades.

In a window of the helicopter Timmy caught a glimpse of a man in a red coat. It was Santa Claus. He had arrived. 'It's Santa Claus!' A great shout went up from the crowd. 'Hurrah!' they cheered. In their excitement they had forgotten their long wait. The band struck up 'Here comes Santa Claus' as the helicopter landed. But with the noise no one could hear the music. The waiting people clutched their hats which would have blown away in the wind from the whirling rotor blades.

The helicopter door opened and Mister Vicious stepped out. He glared at the waiting crowd. Then two other thugs stepped out and took up guard each side of the door.

'Who are they?' Timmy wondered. 'They look like body-guards.' But Santa Claus never had bodyguards before. It was certainly very strange.

The helicopter's rotor blades stopped whirring and there was silence. Mister Mayor and Mister Manager stepped forward. But the thugs barred their way. 'Get back,' Mister Vicious growled threateningly. 'Santa Claus doesn't want to be crowded.'

'But it's tradition,' Mister Mayor protested. 'I'm the most important man in the city. I always welcome Santa Claus.'

'Beat it,' Mister Vicious said. 'And take your necklace with you.'

The crowd laughed. They didn't like Mister Mayor. They thought he was far too pompous. Mister Mayor glared around him. His face was red but his nose glowed purple and blue from the cold. 'I have my speech to make,' he said. 'I spent all last night writing it. I am going to make it and no one can stop me.'

Mister Mayor puffed out his chest and threw back his head. He thought it made him look more important. But he only looked ridiculous. 'Mister Claus,' he began, 'fellow dig-nitaries, ladies and gentlemen and children. It gives me great pleasure to welcome Mister Claus to our great city. Though I am the most important man in the city, it is still a great hon-our for me to welcome him. I am going to present Mister Claus with the freedom of this city of mine. He has only to ask and whatever he wants will be given him. As the most important man I …'

Just then Santa Claus appeared in the doorway of the helicopter. A great cheer went up from the crowd and Mister Mayor's words were drowned out. The children waved and cried out with delight. They didn't know that the man in the red suit wasn't Santa Claus but Mister Carbuncle.

From behind the crowd Timmy Goodfellow watched Santa. There was something wrong. Santa Claus seemed enormously fat. And his face looked decidedly green. Was Santa ill? Had he begun to suffer from airsickness? And where was Rudolph and the sleigh?

Timmy watched as Santa Claus stepped unsteadily onto the concrete. He stumbled and would have fallen if one of the thugs hadn't taken his arm. Timmy could see that Santa's clothes were ill-fitting. He was much too fat for them.

The crowd grew silent. They too were aware that something was not quite right. They watched as Santa Claus took a few unsteady steps. Mister Mayor held out his hand in welcome but Santa Claus brushed it aside. He stopped before Mister Mayor and grabbed his chain of office. 'Is it gold?' Santa asked.

'Oh yes,' Mister Mayor said in a haughty voice. He was very proud of his chain of office. 'And the stones are real rubies and emeralds. This one here is a diamond. It is one of the biggest diamonds in the world.'

'You've just granted me the freedom of the city,' Santa

Claus said. 'You said that I could have anything I want, right?'

'Oh yes,' Mister Mayor said. 'Anything you want. Anything at all.'

'Well, give me that necklace,' Santa Claus demanded. 'I want that.'

'But, but, but …' Mister Mayor stuttered. 'This necklace … I mean this chain is my chain of office. No one else can have it.'

'Give it to me,' Santa Claus ordered in a gruff voice.

But Mister Mayor shook his head. 'I can't,' he whispered. 'It's mine. Mine.' He clutched the chain and shuffled away nervously.

'Get it for me,' Santa Claus ordered and the two thugs moved forward. They grabbed Mister Mayor by the arms and Mister Vicious removed the chain. He took it to Santa Claus and hung it about his neck.

Mister Mayor cried out in anguish. He swayed and fell to the ground. Two dignitaries rushed to his aid and lifted him up. They led him to his black car and bundled him inside, before the car sped away.

Mister Vicious and the two thugs led Santa Claus towards the entrance to Toys Galore. As they reached the steps a little girl ran from the crowd. She had a bunch of flowers, grown specially in her father's greenhouse, to give to Santa Claus. But Mister Vicious caught her by the arm and held her. He grabbed the flowers and threw them on the ground. Then he flung the girl away from him. She would have fallen if her father had not caught her.

The crowd was stunned. They were much too stunned to protest. So they remained silent. Santa Claus mounted the steps. Timmy Goodfellow stepped forward to welcome him. 'Hello again, Santa Claus,' Timmy said. He held out his hand. 'I ...'

But Santa Claus roughly brushed his hand aside and strode past into the store. Behind him strode Mister Manager and his assistants. They all looked worried and concerned.

Timmy followed them. They trooped along to Santa's Cave where Santa Claus threw himself into his chair. Mister Vicious stood beside him. 'Get me a glass of whiskey,' Santa Claus ordered. 'It'll help settle my stomach. It's still upset after the flight in that helicopter.'

'But ...' Mister Manager protested.

'No buts,' Santa Claus shouted. 'Just get me the whiskey.' He glared around him and then began to examine Mister Mayor's chain. 'Real gold,' he said, gloatingly. 'And just look at the size of that diamond.'

Mister Vicious stepped forward to examine the diamond but Santa Claus struck him. 'Don't crowd me,' he barked.

An assistant returned with a large glass of whiskey. Santa Claus gulped it down and wiped his mouth on the sleeve of his coat.

'Are you ready now, Santa Claus?' Mister Manager asked nervously. 'We're an hour late. The children have been waiting so long.'

'Let them wait,' Santa Claus growled.

Mister Manager's face turned pale. 'I'm … I'm sorry,' he mumbled. He turned to Timmy. 'You'd better sit here,' he said. He waved Timmy to his seat at the little table.

'Who's he?' Santa Claus asked angrily.

'This is Timmy Goodfellow,' Mister Manager said. 'He operated your computer last year when Elf Byte was taken ill. Remember?'

'Oh yes,' Santa Claus said slowly. 'That boy. He got everything wrong. I don't want him anywhere near me.'

'But who'll operate the computer?' Mister Manager asked.

'I don't bother with computers any more,' Santa Claus said. 'Now can we get on with this business. I want to start making money. Put that boy outside and get him to keep those children quiet. They're making an awful racket and I hate noise.'

'Go outside,' Mister Manager ordered Timmy. 'Do what Santa Claus says.'

Timmy went outside. His heart was in his boots. He had been so looking forward to meeting Santa. And now he was being treated so badly. Santa Claus was clearly very ill.

There was a large queue of children and their parents waiting outside Santa's Cave. They were all making a lot of noise. 'Be quiet,' Timmy said. 'Santa isn't well.'

The crowd gasped. Then they began to buzz like bees. 'Be

quiet,' Timmy ordered again. 'Please be quiet.' Tears formed in his eyes. But he was a brave lad and didn't cry.

Mister Manager emerged from Santa's Cave. 'He's ready,' he said. 'Send in the first child.'

Timmy sent in a girl and her mother. 'Has anyone a note-book and pen?' he asked.

A woman in the queue gave Timmy a notebook and pen. Timmy listened. The girl told Santa Claus she wanted a doll's house for Christmas. 'Is that all?' Timmy heard Santa Claus say. 'That's not very much. Wouldn't you like a doll too? And furniture for the house? And a pram?'

Timmy couldn't believe his ears. Santa Claus was telling the girl that she could have dozens of presents. It would cost a fortune. Timmy heard the girl's mother protest that she couldn't afford all the presents. But Santa Claus ordered Mister Vicious to take the money from the woman's purse.

Timmy heard the woman cry out and Santa Claus laugh. Then the woman came running out of Santa's Cave. She was crying. The little girl followed. She also was crying.

Timmy was upset. But he wrote the girl's name in his note-book and beside her name he noted that she wanted a doll's house. It was all he could do. Santa Claus was clearly very unwell. He would not remember the details himself. Even if there was no computer, Timmy was still going to do the job Santa Claus had asked him to do last year.

8
Mrs Kindheart and Mrs Needy

Timmy showed the children in to see Santa Claus. As each minute went by Timmy became more convinced that something was wrong. Santa Claus was bad tempered and had no patience at all. 'Speak up, speak up,' he ordered any child who whispered. But when a child did speak up Santa Claus shouted at them not to talk so loudly. He was only happy when a child asked for a lot of very expensive presents. Then Timmy could hear him smacking his lips and mumbling about how much more gold and jewels that meant.

Timmy wrote each child's name in his notebook along with details of what they'd asked for. Then he showed in the next child. Next in the queue was a young woman. Her eyes were red as if she had been crying. She had no children with her. 'You can't go in,' Timmy said. 'Only those with children are allowed in.'

'Please let me go in,' the woman begged. 'I must speak with Santa. He's the only person in the world who can help me.' Her face was thin and the corners of her mouth drooped like a clown's. Her eyes were sad and they pleaded with Timmy.

'Go on,' he said. 'But don't delay. Santa Claus isn't well.'

'Oh thank you,' the woman said. 'Thank you.' She ran into Santa's Cave and threw herself on her knees before Santa. 'Help me, Santa Claus,' she cried. 'Please help me.'

'What's this?' Santa Claus shouted. He pushed the woman away but she clung to his coat.

'Please,' she repeated. 'Please help me.'

Timmy's heart leapt in his chest. He hated to see anyone in distress. But he knew Santa Claus would help the woman. Santa was a kind and gentle man. He loved everyone, even the animals. So Timmy was shocked when Santa tried to push the woman away again. He grabbed at her arms and tore her fingers loose from his coat. 'Get her out of here,' he screamed.

Mister Vicious darted forward. He caught the woman and tried to drag her away. But her fingers had again gripped Santa's coat.

'Pull her by the hair,' Santa Claus shouted. 'Then she'll let go.'

Timmy felt a lump rise in his throat. How could Santa be so cruel? He covered his face with his hands and peered between his fingers.

Mister Vicious caught the woman by the hair and pulled

57

it. She screamed but Mister Vicious wouldn't let go. Slowly the woman's fingers opened and Mister Vicious was able to drag her across the floor and throw her out. She fell at Timmy's feet and Mister Vicious threw a clump of her hair on the ground beside her. It had been pulled out from the roots.

The woman beat her fists on the floor. But everyone was too shocked to help her. It was left to Timmy to comfort her. 'It's all right,' he said. 'Santa is ill. He doesn't know what he's doing.' There were tears in Timmy's eyes but he held them back.

'No one will help me,' the woman wailed.

'Santa will help you,' Timmy said. 'If you tell me what it is you want I'll write it down in my notebook. Santa is bringing me a special present this year but I'll tell him to bring it to your child instead.'

At this the woman began to wail louder and louder. 'I have no child,' she sobbed. 'That's why I wanted to see Santa Claus. I want him to bring me children. I want a little boy and girl of my own.'

'The poor woman,' the waiting people cried. 'Santa Claus is very cruel not to have listened to her. He's a horrible man.'

'No he's not,' Timmy cried out. 'He's a kind ... gentle man. He loves everyone. It's just that he's ... he's sick.' A tear formed at the edge of Timmy's eye and trickled over. It ran slowly down his cheek. He didn't know what to do. The woman still sobbed on the floor. Timmy helped her to her feet. 'Give me your name and address,' he said, 'and I'll write it down.'

'I'm Mrs Kindheart,' the woman said. 'I live at Friendly Cottage. I love children. If Santa Claus could bring me a boy and girl for Christmas I would be very happy.'

'I'll write it down,' Timmy said.

'Thank you,' Mrs Kindheart said. 'I can tell you're a good boy.'

Timmy wrote the details in his notebook. Then he sent a boy into Santa's Cave. But Santa was in foul humour. He hardly listened at all and when the boy had given a list of the presents he wanted, Santa ordered Mister Vicious to throw him out.

Next Timmy sent in a poor woman and her children. She wore ragged clothes and her face was thin and pale from hunger. Her children were dressed in ragged clothes too and their faces and hands were blue with cold. Their shoes were badly worn and their toes peeped out through them.

'My name is Mrs Needy,' the woman said to Santa. 'I have no money. As you can see we are poor. My children have only torn clothes and worn shoes. They are always cold and hungry.'

'What do I care?' Santa Claus growled. 'If you have no money what are you doing here?'

'I was told that you were the kindest man in the world,' Mrs Needy said. 'I hoped you would bring Christmas presents to my poor children.'

'If you've no money,' Santa Claus said, 'how can I bring you anything? Toys cost money. If I were to bring toys to every poor

59

child in the world then I'd have no gold or jewels for myself. I have only one chest filled with gold and jewels. That isn't enough for me. I want more.'

'Please, Santa,' Mrs Needy pleaded. 'Please bring toys to my children. Just a small toy each.'

'Throw her and her children out,' Santa Claus said, 'before she starts breaking my heart with her sob story.' He laughed as Mister Vicious caught two of the children by the ears and threw them out. He caught Mrs Needy by the arm and the third child by the ear and dragged them outside.

'Clear off,' Mister Vicious growled. 'If there are any more of you who can't pay for what you want, you may as well clear off now. Santa Claus has better things to do than listen to poor people.'

He swung about and saw Timmy Goodfellow. He caught Timmy by the ear and tugged hard. 'You should know better than be bothering Santa Claus with the likes of those. Any more like that and you'll feel the weight of my boot.' He glared around him before retreating back into Santa's Cave.

Timmy called Mrs Needy to him and took down her address. He told her Santa Claus was only joking and promised he would still bring her children some nice presents for Christmas. 'Oh thank you,' Mrs Needy said. She gathered her children together and they hurried out.

Timmy Goodfellow was worried now. Something awful certainly had happened. The Santa Claus he knew and loved would never have behaved like that. And he wouldn't have such horrible men with him. Something terrible must have happened to the real Santa Claus. The man in Santa's Cave wasn't the real Santa Claus. He was an impostor!

But who would believe him? And what could he do? Timmy thought hard until sweat appeared on his forehead. But he couldn't think of what he should do. He wanted to show everyone that the man in Santa's Cave was an impostor. But how could he do it?

Timmy sent in more children. Their mother had a baby in her arms and was carrying a shopping bag. The children told Santa what they wanted for Christmas. And then, before Santa could say anything, the woman placed the baby on his lap. 'Take it away,' Santa shouted. 'I don't like babies. They cry all the time and wee on your clothes.'

Mister Vicious rushed to take the baby. But the woman had placed her shopping bag on the floor. Mister Vicious tripped over it and sprawled on his face. The children laughed. Timmy Goodfellow and the waiting parents and children laughed.

'Help!' Santa Claus shouted. 'Help! Get this baby off my lap.' Mister Vicious tried to get up. But one of the children pushed him and he fell on his face again.

'Ah!' Santa Claus wailed. 'The baby has wet me. My trousers are all wet. It's all warm and it's running down my legs. Help!'

Timmy Goodfellow was doubled up with laughter. In fact he had a pain in his stomach from laughing. He could barely watch as the woman took the baby and herself and her children, still laughing, went out of Santa's Cave.

From the corner of his eye Timmy Goodfellow could see Santa Claus. His face was as red as a beetroot. There was froth coming out of his nostrils. He struggled to his feet and kicked Mister Vicious.

'It's all your fault,' he cried in temper. 'It was your suggestion we kidnap Santa Claus and that I should take his place. You promised me I would get lots of gold and jewels. And all I've had so far is poor women without money and babies that wee on my trousers.'

He kicked Mister Vicious again and again. 'I'm hungry and tired,' he said. 'I need to rest. I want a large glass of whiskey, a fat cigar and two bowls of ice-cream. Get up and get them for me this minute.'

Mister Vicious crawled out of range of Santa's boot. He scuttled out. Santa then sat down again and glared about him.

Timmy Goodfellow had no longer any doubt. The imposter in Santa's Cave had kidnapped the real Santa Claus. But who was he and where did he come from? And where was the real Santa Claus? He had an idea how he might find out who the imposter was and quietly he slipped away. He left the store and went out to where the helicopter was waiting.

9
Eggs and Tomatoes

Timmy Goodfellow went out to where one of the thugs was guarding the helicopter. 'Excuse me, sir,' Timmy said.

'Yeah.' The thug had a cruel twisted mouth. Tufts of hair stuck out of his ears and nostrils. They were like the bristles on the broom Timmy used to sweep the floors at Mrs Haggard's house.

'Please, sir,' Timmy said, 'Mister Manager sent me.'

'What's he want?' The thug swung towards Timmy and clenched his fists.

Timmy was frightened. But he was a brave lad and stood his ground. If he didn't do something then Christmas was doomed. 'Please, sir,' he said, 'Mister Manager needs the name and address so that he can send on the fee.'

'Name and address? Fee?' The thug screwed up his face as

he tried to figure it out. But he had never gone to school and was very ignorant. He couldn't write his name and honestly thought that two and two made five.

'Mister Manager always pays Santa Claus a large fee each year,' Timmy said. 'He's asked me to get the name and address, so he can send on the bag of gold pieces.'

'Gold pieces did you say?' The thug's eyes glowed with greed.

'Oh yes,' Timmy said enthusiastically. 'It's a big heavy bag. Even I couldn't lift it. Mister Manager says the gold is to be shared with all Santa's helpers, so you will get lots of gold pieces yourself.'

Now the thug's eyes glowed even brighter. 'How many pieces will I get?' he asked.

'A hundred pieces,' Timmy said.

'Is that more than five?' the thug asked.

'Oh yes,' Timmy said. 'You'll have enough gold to fill your pockets to the brim. Now all Mister Manager needs is the name and address.'

'He must deliver it to Mister Carbuncle,' the thug said. 'The address is The Thieves' Den, The Underworld.'

'Oh!' It was all Timmy could say. He stared at the thug with wide-open, scared eyes. Timmy could hardly believe the man who was pretending to be Santa Claus was Mister Carbuncle. He was such a well-known cruel and evil man.

Timmy had heard he ate little boys for his breakfast.

'Well?' the thug growled.

'Wha … what?' Timmy managed to ask.

'Get going. Before I give you the toe of my boot.' The thug showed Timmy his boots. They had great shiny steel toecaps. 'Go on. Give Mister Manager the name and address.'

'Name?' Timmy said. 'Address? Oh yes. I'd best run,' he added nervously. 'I don't want to keep Mister Carbuncle waiting for his gold.'

Timmy Goodfellow ran back into Toys Galore. He ran down a long hallway into the huge room where all the toys were stored. It was quiet here and he had time to think. He could hardly believe the man in the Santa Claus suit was Mister Carbuncle. To think he had stood beside him! What if Mister Carbuncle took a liking to him and wanted to eat him for breakfast?

Timmy shivered and his teeth chattered. But he grabbed his hair in his hands and tugged until it hurt. He wasn't going to be frightened. Instead he was going to teach Mister Carbuncle and his thugs a lesson. Timmy became determined. He gritted his teeth and clenched his fists.

He ran out of Toys Galore, along to Mister Greengrocer's shop. The boy who worked in the shop was Timmy's friend. Timmy told the boy what he was going to do.

'Have you got any rotten tomatoes?' Timmy asked.

'We've got lots,' Timmy's friend said.

'Can I have some, please?' Timmy asked.

The boy gave Timmy six boxes of rotten tomatoes. 'We have six cartons of rotten eggs too,' the boy said and Timmy's face lit up. Rotten eggs were best of all.

The boy helped Timmy carry the boxes and cartons to the store. Timmy thanked him and then went along to where the children were waiting outside Santa's Cave. Timmy whispered to the children and a buzz went through the store. The children let go of their parents' hands and followed Timmy to the door. Quickly Timmy handed out the rotten tomatoes. To the bigger children he gave handfuls of rotten eggs.

'We're going to surprise Santa Claus,' Timmy said. 'He loves to see children enjoying themselves. He'll be delighted when we attack him and his helpers with all the rotten things.'

The children were very excited. Even the little ones who couldn't throw anything offered to carry extra tomatoes and eggs for their bigger brothers and sisters. They milled around the door waiting for the signal from Timmy.

He had filled his pockets with rotten eggs. Now he took as many as he could carry in his hands. Quickly, he looked around his assembled army. 'Ready?' he called out.

'Ready,' they chorused.

'Forward,' Timmy ordered and he led them into the store. Mister Manager saw the crowd of advancing children and was horrified. He rushed forward to stop them but they brushed him aside. They marched up through the store while their parents watched in complete surprise. Bravely, Timmy led them to Santa's Cave. 'Halt,' he ordered. He stepped forward and pulled back the flap. Mister Carbuncle was sitting on Santa's chair. He had a glass of whiskey in his hand and a cigar stuck between his rubbery lips.

Mister Vicious stood beside him with a cigar lighter and a bottle of whiskey. It was his job to relight the cigar if it went out and to refill Mister Carbuncle's glass.

'What's this?' Mister Carbuncle roared. 'Can't you see that I'm busy? Get out of here. Get that boy,' he ordered Mister Vicious. 'See to it that you teach him a lesson he won't easily forget.'

Timmy Goodfellow hesitated. What he was about to do could get him into serious trouble. But then he thought of his friend Santa Claus. These terrible thugs had him locked up somewhere. Santa would be cold and hungry and lonely.

'Now!' Timmy shouted, as loud as he could. He threw the first egg and it hit the glowing tip of Mister Carbuncle's cigar. Sparks flew everywhere and the cigar was pushed deep into Mister Carbuncle's mouth. The lighted tip touched his false beard and it began to singe.

'Help!' Mister Carbuncle cried out, leaping to his feet. 'Help! Help!' He tore at his beard and some of it came away in his hands. It was stained with the yolk of the egg which splashed everywhere. The smell was awful.

Timmy's second egg hit Mister Carbuncle on the nose. Mister Carbuncle yelped as the egg broke and splattered his face. 'Get him,' he screamed at Mister Vicious. 'Or I'll have you whipped.'

Mister Vicious dropped the whiskey bottle and it shattered. The whiskey spilled out on the floor. 'You clumsy oaf,' Mister Carbuncle screamed. 'That's my whiskey you've spilt. I'll have you flogged.' He jumped up and down and pulled at his beard in anger.

But before Mister Vicious could rush forward, the children began to pelt him and Mister Carbuncle with rotten eggs and tomatoes. The two thugs tried to protect themselves but the rotten tomatoes and eggs seemed to come from everywhere. 'Stop them! Stop them!' Mister Carbuncle roared at the top of his voice. But there was nothing Mister Vicious could do.

'Run!' he shouted. 'Run for your life.' He turned and ran towards the back of Santa's Cave and scuttled out through the rear exit.

'Coward!' Mister Carbuncle roared even louder. 'I'll have your nails pulled out with a pincers. I'll … ah!' Mister Carbuncle had opened his mouth too wide. Timmy Goodfellow had taken careful aim and thrown a rotten egg. It hit Mister Carbuncle full in the mouth and broke. All the slimy yellow yolk ran down Mister Carbuncle's chin and onto what remained of his beard.

'You'll pay for this,' he spluttered, holding his nose because the smell was terrible. But he knew that for the present he was beaten. Quickly he turned on his heels and scuttled after Mister Vicious.

'Forward,' Timmy Goodfellow ordered, wild with excitement. 'Let's get him.' He rushed round the back of Santa's Cave, followed by the whooping, cheering children.

Mister Vicious and Mister Carbuncle ran to the exit and out to where the helicopter was waiting. 'Get us out of here! Get us out of here!' both thugs were shouting at the top of their voices.

Timmy Goodfellow and the children followed. They threw the rotten tomatoes and eggs which poured down on the two thugs like hailstones. The thugs reached the helicopter and both tried to climb on board at the same time. They pushed and they pulled. They shoved and they jostled. Mister Vicious had almost climbed into the helicopter. But Mister Carbuncle caught him by the legs and pulled him back out. They began to struggle. They kicked and scratched one another. Then Mister Carbuncle fell over.

The safety pins holding the seams of his trousers burst open. The trousers split and fell down. Mister Carbuncle's face got very red. He grabbed at his trousers and tried to pull them up.

The children roared with laughter. Even Timmy Goodfellow had to stop throwing the rotten eggs. There were tears in his eyes from laughing and he had to stop to wipe them away.

The thugs took advantage of the lull. Mister Vicious scrambled into the helicopter, and leaned out and pulled Mister Carbuncle up. His trousers were around his knees and his enormous bottom stuck up in the air. He got caught in the doorway but somehow Mister Vicious managed to drag him inside. The engine roared into life and slowly the rotor blades whirled. Faster and faster they whirred until they were just a blur. Slowly the helicopter lifted off from the ground.

Inside there was pandemonium. Mister Carbuncle hit out at his fellow thugs. 'Fools!' he shouted. 'Fools! To allow a group of children to make you flee. Cowards! Fools!' He knocked Mister Vicious out of his way and sat down. But he'd forgotten that the pins holding the seams of his trousers together were open. The sharp ends of the pins prodded Mister Carbuncle's fat bottom.

'Ah,' he screeched. 'Oh!' He jumped up and down and up and down as the helicopter tilted and headed across the rooftops of the city towards The Thieves' Den.

10
Timmy Escapes

*A*s the helicopter took off Mister Manager rushed from the store and grabbed Timmy Goodfellow by the ear. 'You horrible boy,' he said. 'Look what you've done.'

'Ouch!' Timmy groaned. 'Let me go.'

'Horrible! Horrible!' Mister Manager jumped up and down. Each time he jumped up in the air he pulled Timmy's ear. 'I'm ruined. Ruined!' He let go of Timmy and wrung his hands. 'Santa will never come here again. I just know he won't. We'll have no more money. My wife and children will starve. We'll be ruined. Ruined!'

Timmy took the opportunity to move away from Mister Manager. 'That wasn't Santa Claus,' he said. 'That was Mister Carbuncle, The Boss of The Underworld. He's kidnapped Santa Claus and taken his place.'

71

'Lies!' Mister Manager screamed. 'How dare you tell me such lies.'

'But it's true,' Timmy said. 'You must call the police and tell them that Santa Claus has been kidnapped by those cruel men.'

'Lies,' Mister Manager screamed again. It seemed as if it were the only word he knew. 'All lies. You've ruined every-thing.'

By now a large crowd of parents had gathered around Mister Manager and Timmy. The other children had slipped away. Timmy was on his own.

'There he is.' A shout went up from the crowd. 'There's that horrible boy.'

Timmy could see that the parents were very angry. They had red faces and were stamping their feet. He was scared. But only for a moment.

'Listen to me,' he called out. 'That man was an impostor. He wasn't the real Santa Claus at all.'

'Maybe he's right,' a man said. 'He didn't behave like Santa Claus.'

'Rubbish!' Mister Manager said and a murmur of agreement went up from all the other people. 'This horrible boy here has ruined everyone's day. To think that he insulted Santa Claus, the kindest man in the whole world.'

The man in the crowd who'd supported Timmy opened his

mouth to speak again. But the crowd growled in anger and the man quickly shut his mouth. He looked about him and quietly slipped away.

Mister Manager and the crowd were getting angrier. They crushed about Timmy in a threatening manner. Men shook fists and made growling noises. Timmy could feel their hot breath on his face.

'Go!' Mister Manager pointed with his finger. 'Go, you horrible boy! Don't ever come back here again.'

'But my money,' Timmy protested. 'You owe me money. I need it to buy food for myself and my sister.'

'You can both starve,' Mister Manager said cruelly.

'But my little sister,' Timmy whispered. 'She …'

'Let her cry,' Mister Manager said. 'I'm sure she's a horrible child just like you.'

'She's not!' Timmy couldn't bear anyone to say anything against Katie. He rushed at Mister Manager with his fists clenched. But Mister Assistant caught him by the arms and held him.

'See what kind of boy he is,' Mister Manager said. 'He's not only horrible but violent too. I'm going to call the police and have him thrown in jail.'

The crowd began to yell in agreement. As Timmy looked about he could see a ring of threatening faces.

'You'd best run,' Mister Assistant said to Timmy. He knew

the crowd would set upon the boy in a moment and he hated the sight of blood.

Timmy realised he was beaten. No one would believe him now. And if the crowd were to pounce on him and beat him he would have to go to the hospital. Katie would be alone with the horrible Mrs Haggard. And if the crowd didn't beat him the police would throw him in jail. He might never see Katie again.

Timmy turned about and ducked his head. He dashed forward. All he could see before him were the legs of the crowd. Hands grabbed him but he twisted this way and that. Someone caught his hair but he wrenched his head free. Some of his hair was torn out, but he ignored the pain. In a moment he reached the edge of the crowd and was free.

He ran as fast as his legs would carry him. Behind him he heard the clatter of footsteps as the crowd pursued him. But he ducked and weaved and managed to avoid their grasp. He ran and ran. But still the crowd pursued him. He was weak from hunger and began to tire. Behind him he could hear the clatter of the running feet getting closer and closer.

Soon he heard their heavy breathing. They were right behind him. A hand caught the tail of his anorak. But he managed to put on a spurt of speed and it took him out of reach. He knew he couldn't evade them forever though. They would soon catch him. His heart was beating faster and faster.

Timmy had left the city centre and was now in the part where the poorer people lived. The streets were very narrow and the houses were small with low doors and tiny windows. There were no cars because the people were so poor that they couldn't afford them. Timmy turned down one of the narrow streets. Behind him the crowd still followed. He ran down this street and that. He twisted and turned. But the crowd still pursued him.

He followed a narrow alleyway. It was so narrow that the crowd following him got caught in the entrance. While they jostled each other Timmy gained some ground. He turned the next corner and a boy dashed from a doorway. Timmy tried to duck but the boy caught his elbow.

'This way,' he whispered urgently. 'Follow me.'

Timmy couldn't even think any more. He followed the boy. They turned and twisted through a maze of narrow alleys. The boy turned another corner and dashed through the open door of a deserted house. Timmy followed him.

The boy looked earnestly at Timmy and placed a finger against his lips. 'Shhh,' the boy said. Tensed up, they listened. They heard the crowd draw near. Holding their breaths, they heard the mob rush past. They sounded like a troop of charging elephants. The boys listened until the noise died down.

'It's safe now,' the boy said to Timmy. 'You can come with me.'

Timmy followed the boy. He led Timmy through the web of back streets. Once, they heard the crowd baying in the distance. Timmy stopped to listen but the boy beckoned him urgently. Eventually they made their way out of this part of the city. Timmy now knew where he was. 'You'll be safe now,' the boy said. 'The crowd have gone the other way.'

'Who are you?' Timmy asked. 'Why did you help me?'

'I'm Mrs Needy's son, Teddy,' the boy said. 'You were kind to us today when we went to visit Santa Claus. I recognised you when I saw the crowd following you. So I helped you in turn.'

'Thank you very much,' Timmy said. He shook hands with the boy and then headed for Mrs Haggard's house. His heart wasn't beating so fast now. Instead it felt very heavy. He had failed to persuade Mister Manager that Santa Claus was an impostor. So even now, Santa Claus was being held prisoner. Timmy Goodfellow had let Santa down.

Timmy's heart grew sadder with every step. He had failed Santa Claus. He had failed Katie. He had failed all the people who had come to the store today. He'd failed Mrs Kindheart and Mrs Needy and her children. The salt of Timmy's tears was in his eyes but he wouldn't cry. Timmy Goodfellow would never cry again.

11
Mister Carbuncle is Airsick

Mister Carbuncle and Mister Vicious smelled like a dung heap. They were holding their noses and trying to clean the mess off their clothes. The rotten egg was runny and sticky. It matted hair. It dribbled into pockets. It ran up arms and trickled down trouser legs. 'Help me to clean this mess,' Mister Carbuncle screamed.

The thugs tried to clean the mess but Mister Carbuncle hit out at them. 'Fools!' he cried. 'Why do I ever listen to fools?'

'It's not our fault,' they wailed. 'The idea was Mister Illegal's.'

'I'll have him fried in oil,' Mister Carbuncle said. 'I'll have him skinned alive.' With each word he hit the thugs on the head with his fists.

'Ouch!' they screamed. 'Ouch! Ouch! Ouch!'

'You are useless,' Mister Carbuncle said. 'You can't do anything. And look! I'm still covered in rotten egg and tomato.' He struck them and it pleased him to see them cringe before him. 'I'm very tired now,' he added. 'I must sit down.'

He sat in his comfortable seat but he'd forgotten that the safety pins were still open. Once again the sharp ends stuck in his fat bottom. He leapt from his seat. Now it was his turn to cry 'Ouch! Ouch! Ouch!' He grabbed at his sore bottom and pulled the pins out.

'Oh,' he bellowed. 'Ah.' He danced around but he was so fat and heavy that he upset the helicopter. It swung this way and that way. Mister Carbuncle lost his footing. He fell into another seat. Yet again the pins stuck in his bottom.

He screamed and leapt up again. But the helicopter tilted the other way and he fell into another seat. Again and again he fell and each time the pins stuck into him. He yelped and jumped and screamed. He cried like a baby. He put his thumb in his mouth and began to suck it.

The other thugs couldn't help themselves and they laughed. They laughed until they got pains in their bellies. Tears streamed down their faces. They roared with delight as they watched Mister Carbuncle dance here, there and everywhere.

'Oh the pins,' he wailed. 'Pull out the pins.'

It was a full ten minutes before the thugs stopped laughing.

78

Then Mister Vicious stepped forward and began to remove the pins. 'Ouch! Ouch! Ouch!' Mister Carbuncle cried as each pin was removed. 'Oh the pain,' he cried. 'Oh, the terrible pain!'

Mister Vicious pulled out the last pin and Mister Carbuncle was able to sit down. He glared about at his henchmen.

'Wait until I get back to The Thieves' Den,' he threatened. 'I'll have you all whipped. I'll have you all fried in oil. I'll ...'

Suddenly Mister Carbuncle's face turned green. He'd eaten too much ice-cream and drunk too much whiskey. Now, with the movement of the helicopter, he felt sick. His eyes rolled about in his head. His stomach heaved. He became greener and greener.

Just as suddenly as he turned green, he got sick. He threw up all the ice-cream and whiskey. It splattered over the thugs. Now it was Mister Carbuncle's turn to laugh. He laughed and laughed while the thugs tried to clean themselves.

Mister Carbuncle was still laughing when the helicopter landed at The Thieves' Den. He immediately went inside and took off Santa's clothes. Then he had a bath and went down to his cellar to count his gold and jewels. But when he saw that the second chest was only half full, tears sprang to his eyes. He had to get more gold and jewels. Otherwise he was going to be very unhappy.

While Mister Carbuncle had been pretending to be Santa Claus, the real Santa Claus was tied up in the aircraft hanger. He desperately tried to undo the ropes which bound him. But they were tied much too tightly and he failed.

'Can you get loose from your bonds, Rudolph?' he asked.

'I've tried, Santa Claus,' Rudolph said. 'But the ropes on my feet are also tied very tightly. I can hardly move at all.'

'Will we ever get out of here?' Santa Claus wondered. 'If we don't those evil men will take over Christmas. People will think I'm a very bad man. They will never trust me again. This will be the last Christmas ever.'

'Don't be upset, Santa Claus,' Rudolph said. 'Timmy Goodfellow will know that the man who kidnapped us is an impostor. He will come and rescue us.'

'Do you think so?' Santa Claus asked.

'I'm certain of it,' Rudolph said. 'Timmy Goodfellow is a fine young boy. Look how he helped you last year. He never made one mistake.'

'That's true,' Santa Claus said. 'He is a fine boy. I know he will do everything he can to help us.'

Santa Claus was encouraged again. He knew that Timmy would do his level best. So Santa began to wriggle and wiggle. He twisted and turned as he tried to escape from the ropes. He loosened the one around his wrists. He could now move his hand a little. He worked on the rope until he got his hand free. Just then he heard a laugh. He swung around and saw one of the thugs who had been left behind to guard him and Rudolph.

'Haw, haw, haw,' the thug chuckled. 'You thought you were going to get away, did you?'

'You'll pay for this,' Santa Claus shouted. 'I think you had better let me go immediately.'

'Not me,' the thug said. 'If I let you go Mister Carbuncle would have me whipped. You must stay here until Mister Carbuncle says you can go. Now, I have to tie you up again.'

The thug walked over to Santa and retied the ropes on his wrists. This time he tied them tighter than ever. No matter how Santa Claus tried, he couldn't move his hands at all. If Timmy Goodfellow didn't come to the rescue, he and Rudolph would never escape.

Mister Manager returned to his store when he and the chasing crowd lost Timmy Goodfellow.

'He's got away from me this time,' Mister Manager said. 'But I'll get him the next time.' He stared around his usually tidy store. It had been turned upside down. There were boxes of toys strewn everywhere. Other toys lay on the floor in pieces. His staff stood around in a daze. There was a rotten tomato stuck to everything. Slimy yellow rotten egg dribbled down the walls. The smell was awful.

'That … that boy,' Mister Manager snarled between his teeth. 'He must be taught a lesson.' Mister Manager took a handkerchief from his pocket and placed it over his nose. He turned to go to his office. But the floor was slippery. His feet slid from under him and he fell down into a pool of horrible foul-smelling goo. His staff couldn't help laughing at him.

'How dare you laugh at me,' he shouted, as he got up. 'How dare you!' He turned around angrily. 'I want this mess cleared up,' he yelled. 'I want my store looking like new. Don't just stand there. Get to it!'

The staff hurriedly found brooms and mops and scrubbing brushes. While they set about cleaning the store, Mister Manager stalked into the washroom and cleaned the mess from his clothes. Then he returned to his office and sat in his big leather chair behind his big wooden desk. He placed his head in his hands and wondered how he might avenge himself on Timmy Goodfellow.

12
Enter Beaky, Robbey, Chirpy and Chalky

Timmy Goodfellow was very sad by the time he reached Mrs Haggard's house. He had forgotten about the chase and how frightened he had been. But he was thankful to the boy who had helped him escape. He let himself in by the back door. Mrs Haggard would not allow him to use the front door. She was worried that Timmy would dirty her fine hall carpet. Timmy knew how to enter the house without being heard and Mrs Haggard, who was always prowling around, didn't hear him arrive.

Timmy crept up the stairs to the attic. He didn't know what he was going to say to Katie. How could he tell her that those thugs had kidnapped Santa Claus? How could he tell her he had failed his kind old friend? How could he tell her he had lost his job at the store and now had no money to buy their food?

At the top of the narrow flight of stairs Timmy hesitated. He didn't have the courage to face Katie. But she must have heard him.

'Is that you, Timmy?' Katie called.

'Yes, Katie,' Timmy replied awkwardly.

'Oh, please come in Timmy,' Katie said. 'I want to hear all about Santa Claus. Oh do come and tell me.' Her voice was filled with excitement.

Timmy's face fell. How could he tell her the truth? It would break her heart. He could imagine the tears running down her pale cheeks. Oh those cruel men! How could they do such a thing? Didn't they know how they were hurting so many children? How could they make it a miserable Christmas for so many?

Timmy opened the door to Katie's room. She was sitting up in bed. Her eyes were open wide with excitement. There was a touch of red colour in her cheeks today. Timmy knew that if only she could get out, the sun would soon make her cheeks as rosy red as they once were.

'Oh Timmy,' she said breathlessly, 'I can't wait to hear all about it. Did you ask Santa Claus to come and visit me like you promised? I spent all afternoon brushing my hair so I would look my best. Do you think I look my best now, Timmy?'

'Oh yes, Katie,' Timmy said. 'You look lovely.'

'I'm going to tell Santa Claus all about you,' Katie said. 'I know that when he hears all you've been doing for me he'll give you a special present for Christmas too.'

'It's ...' Timmy said. 'You see ...' He stared helplessly about. 'I've got bad news,' he eventually managed to blurt out.

'Oh!' Katie said. Her eyes lost their sparkle and her face looked sad. 'Santa Claus can't come to visit me. Is that it Timmy?'

Timmy could only nod his head. 'I bet he's much too busy,' Katie added. 'But it doesn't matter. I knew he would be busy. Maybe next year when I can walk again you'll take me to see him. Will you do that, Timmy?'

Timmy nodded. But inside he felt very sad. If Katie didn't have her operation then she would never walk again. She would never be able to visit Santa Claus by then anyway, because there wouldn't be a Santa Claus any more. When Mister Carbuncle and his thugs had finished, no one would ever trust Santa again. There would be no more Christmas.

Katie noticed that Timmy was sad. 'It doesn't matter, Timmy,' she insisted. 'I don't mind if Santa Claus can't come to see me. I know he'll still bring me a special present. And he'll bring you one too. You'll see.'

'He won't,' Timmy cried. 'He won't. There's no Santa any

more. There won't ever be a Santa again. Those terrible men …'

Katie reached out her hand and touched Timmy on the shoulder. 'What happened today, Timmy?' she asked. 'Please tell me.'

'It's terrible,' Timmy said. He shook his head, and sat on the edge of the bed and told Katie what had happened. 'I've let Santa Claus down,' he added. 'I told him I was his friend. I promised I would help him. But I've let those terrible men get away. Now they'll go to another store tomorrow and take all the money. There won't be presents for any children on Christmas Eve. All the children in the world will be unhappy on Christmas morning and it's all my fault.'

'No, it's not your fault,' Katie said reassuringly. 'You did your best. Oh how I wish I had been there to see those thugs covered in rotten eggs and tomatoes! I wouldn't have been able to stop laughing.'

'It was funny,' Timmy smiled. 'I hit Mister Carbuncle on the tip of his big red nose with an egg. The egg burst and all the slimy, smelly yoke ran down his face and dribbled off the end of his false beard.' He laughed and Katie laughed with him.

'There,' Katie said warmly. 'You're not unhappy any more. You're feeling much better, aren't you?'

'I don't know,' Timmy replied. 'I've lost my job at the store and now I've no money to buy food. We'll be hungry and cold for the whole winter.'

'I don't care,' Katie said bravely. 'I don't mind being hungry and cold. We mustn't be selfish, Timmy. We must think of poor Santa Claus. He's probably in a cold dark room now. You must find him, Timmy, and rescue him.'

'Yes,' Timmy agreed. 'You're right. I must find Santa Claus and rescue him from those thugs.' He became excited, then frowned. 'But how?' he asked. 'I don't know where he is. And all those thugs are big and strong. They're violent. If anything happened to me then you would be all alone in the world.'

'Nothing will happen to you, Timmy,' Katie said. 'Anyone who helps Santa Claus will be all right.'

'But how can I find Santa Claus?' Timmy asked. 'The thugs will have hidden him away. It's a very big city and he could be hidden anywhere.'

'We must get our friends to help us,' Katie suggested.

'Our friends?' Timmy was puzzled.

'The birds and the animals,' Katie said. 'We'll get them to help you find and rescue Santa Claus. Isn't that a great idea, Timmy?'

'Yes.' Timmy nodded vigorously.

'I know you're very brave,' Katie said encouragingly. 'You aren't afraid of those thugs. You'll rescue Santa Claus and save Christmas.'

'We must begin our search now,' Timmy said. 'There's no time to lose. I will call Beaky Blackbird, Robbey Robin, Chirpy Sparrow and Chalky Crow this very minute. They can tell all the other birds.' Timmy hurried to the attic window and opened it. He gave a special whistle and waited. Then he whistled again.

Chirpy Sparrow was nodding off to sleep on the branch of a tree when he heard the whistle.

'That's my friend, Timmy,' he said to himself, taking his head out from beneath his wing. 'Why is he calling this late? And he's also calling Beaky and Robbey and Chalky. I'd best tell them and we'll go and see what Timmy wants.'

Chirpy woke Beaky, Robbey and Chalky. They stretched their wings and yawned.

'Do you know what time it is, Mister Sparrow?' Beaky asked. He was always very formal when he was woken from his sleep.

'I do,' Chirpy said. 'But our friend Timmy Goodfellow has just called us. I think he must be in trouble.'

'Well, why didn't you say so at first?' Beaky asked.' If Timmy is in trouble we must help him. Come on! What's the delay? Let's go.'

The birds flew out of the tree and over to the house. Timmy had left the window open and they flew right in.

'Now what's this trouble you're in, Timmy?' Beaky asked.

'Out with it. I'll soon have it sorted for you.'

'Sit down,' Timmy suggested, 'and I'll tell you.'

The birds perched on the end of the bed and Timmy told them the whole story.

'This is a right how-do-you-do, indeed,' Beaky said. 'Now what are we going to do?'

'We want you to search for Santa Claus,' Katie said. 'You must ask all the birds if they saw him. Someone must have seen Santa.'

'You leave it to us,' Beaky said. 'We'll start our search at dawn. In the meantime I'll have a word with Hooty Owl. He goes out at night and can see in the dark. He can begin searching now.'

'Great,' Timmy and Katie said together. 'And while you're searching we're going to talk to our friends the mice. They can get all their friends to help in the search too.'

'Well, come on then,' Beaky said authoritatively. 'We can't sit here all night. Let's go and find Hooty Owl. There's no time to lose.' The birds bid farewell and flew out the window.

'Now,' Timmy said to Katie, 'I'll call Mousey Mouse. As Beaky said, there's no time to lose.'

13
Mousey and Ratty Take a Hand

Mousey Mouse was very old and had heard of many cruel things in his life. But he had never before heard of anything so cruel as the story Timmy told him. Mousey's whiskers quivered and his tail wriggled.

'We must find Santa Claus,' Mousey insisted. 'Maybe Mister Carbuncle has hidden him in the cellar of The Thieves' Den. I've heard tell it's a big cellar with dark, damp rooms. No mouse has been there in years. Mister Carbuncle hates mice and rats, and has traps with jagged teeth set everywhere.'

'Oh the cruel man,' Katie said, shocked. 'How could he do such a thing?'

'I've heard many stories of the cruel things he does,' Mousey said. 'But we must be brave. We must find Santa Claus and rescue him. I will go to The Thieves' Den and

90

search there.'

'I'm coming with you,' Timmy said.

'It'll be dangerous,' Mousey warned. 'There'll be large traps there too. They'll be large enough to catch a boy your size.'

'I don't care,' Timmy said. 'I have to help you.'

'Be careful,' Katie said nervously. 'Santa Claus would be upset if anything happened to either of you.'

'We'll be careful,' Timmy reassured his sister.

'Most certainly,' Mousey added. 'I'm always careful. I've lived a long life and I want to enjoy my retirement and my grandmice. They visit me each day and bring me gifts of cheese.'

'I'm sure you're a good grandfather,' Katie said, smiling.

'We'd best get going,' Mousey said gruffly. He became embarrassed when anyone praised him. It seemed unfitting for an old mouse like him. 'Are you ready, Timmy?'

'I'm ready,' Timmy replied. He slipped Mousey into his pocket leaving his head sticking out so he could breathe comfortably. Timmy crept downstairs, careful not to make any noise. He wanted to avoid Mrs Haggard. He reached the hall and was about to slip into the kitchen and out the back door when Mrs Haggard appeared.

'It's you, you horrid boy,' Mrs Haggard snapped. 'Sneaking about the house like a mouse, are you? I'll have to set a trap like those with the jagged teeth I set for the mice.'

'Eeekkk!' Timmy heard Mousey draw in his breath fast.

'What was that?' Mrs Haggard demanded. 'I could have sworn I heard a mouse squeak.'

'It was me,' Timmy said, sniffling through his nose, trying to make a noise like Mousey. Timmy felt Mousey snuggle down deep in the pocket.

'Well, stop that, boy!' Mrs Haggard shouted. 'Now, there's no wood for the fire. So go out and chop some.'

'But it's dark,' Timmy protested.

'I don't care,' Mrs Haggard insisted. 'Just go and do it.'

Timmy hung his head and went out. But once he was outside his head shot up as high as a stallion's. He was only pretending to be upset for Mrs Haggard's sake. If he had readily agreed to chop the wood she would have been suspicious.

Once outside Timmy crept across the back yard to the small gate in the hedge. Mousey crept out of Timmy's pocket and scrambled onto his shoulder beside his ear.

'We'll have to be careful,' Timmy said. 'Mister Manager is looking for me.' Quickly he told Mousey what had happened at the store.

'We will have to take care then,' Mousey said. 'It might be best if we didn't go along the streets. You wait here, Timmy, and I'll be back shortly.'

Before Timmy could speak, Mousey slid to the ground and

slipped out through the hedge. Timmy heard a rustle and his friend was gone.

It was cold and the sky was clear. The stars were like the diamonds Timmy had often seen in Mister Jeweller's window. He wanted Katie to have jewels and nice things like their mother once had. But she would never have nice things while she lived with Mrs Haggard.

In the distance Timmy heard an owl hoot. It was answered by two more hoots. Then he heard the beat of wings as they flew above him and he caught a glimpse of them as they crossed the face of the moon. Beaky had got his friends the owls to look for Santa Claus just as he had promised.

Timmy felt a surge of hope. With the birds and animals on his side he would find Santa Claus, he felt sure. But how was he to rescue him from the thugs of The Underworld? As Mousey had said, they were dangerous and cruel men. They wouldn't let Santa Claus go without a fight.

Just then he heard a rustle at his feet. It was Mousey.

'Come with me, Timmy,' Mousey whispered. 'Through the gap in the hedge over here.'

Timmy crawled through the narrow gap and found himself in the field adjoining Mrs Haggard's house. Mousey led the way across the field and Timmy followed, the moonlight throwing their shadows before them. They crossed a number of fields and then crawled through a gap in another hedge.

They could see dark warehouses and factories with towering chimneys like fingers pointing at the moon. Mousey led Timmy across a puddled yard to the rear of one of the factories.

'See that grating?' Mousey asked. 'I want you to open it.'

The iron grating was set in the ground beneath Timmy's feet. He stooped down and tugged at the bars. They were rusted and it took many pulls to loosen. Timmy removed it and stared into the dark opening.

'You'll be Timmy Goodfellow,' a voice said from the darkness.

Timmy strained his eyes but couldn't see anything. 'I'm Timmy,' he said.

'I'm Ratty Rat,' the voice said. 'Your friend Mousey has asked me to help you. Now you must climb down here to me.'

Timmy was about to speak when he felt Mousey run up his trouser leg and scramble onto his shoulder.

'Shhh,' Mousey said in Timmy's ear. 'Ratty can be temperamental. Don't say anything.'

'But I thought mice and rats didn't like each other,' Timmy whispered.

'Ratty and myself are old,' Mousey said. 'We don't have time for all that squabbling. We meet once a week to discuss affairs. We talk about our families and of how it used to be in the old days. Now let's not delay or we'll upset Ratty and he'll become grumpy.'

Timmy nodded and put Mousey into his pocket. Then he slipped through the opening, and found himself in a small room hardly bigger than a cupboard. It was gloomy but a glow came from below. As his eyes became accustomed to the gloom, Timmy could see a flight of stairs leading downwards towards the glow of light.

Timmy went down the stone stairs. His shoes made a rapping sound which echoed back to him. As he neared the bottom of the stairs he saw an old grey rat holding a burning torch in his paw.

'These are the old city sewers,' Ratty said. 'They lead right to the cellar of The Thieves' Den. Follow me and I'll take you there.'

Timmy followed Ratty. The tunnel was built of brick and was crumbling away. It was damp and cold and his footsteps echoed much louder now. The tunnel led into another tunnel and then another. At one time they came to a place where many tunnels met. Timmy didn't have any idea where he was.

But Ratty knew his way. He didn't hesitate. He took a tunnel to his left and moved forward. Timmy kept his eye on the torch. It stopped moving and Timmy came up to Ratty.

'Can you see that grill?' Ratty asked. He held up the torch and Timmy could see the iron grill. 'It leads into the very room where Mister Carbuncle keeps his gold and jewels.'

He beckoned Timmy forward and shone the torch through the grill. Timmy could see two great chests.

'One of them is filled with gold and jewels,' Ratty said. 'The other is half full. But Mister Carbuncle isn't satisfied. He wants more and more. I have seen him counting it all greedily.'

'I know,' Timmy said. 'It's why he kidnapped Santa Claus. He wants to take over Christmas and keep all the money for himself. Would you know, Mister Rat, if Santa Claus is here?'

'I'm afraid I wouldn't,' Ratty said. 'You see, Mister Carbuncle has all kinds of traps set. We never venture in there any more. Look. There is one of his traps.'

Timmy looked. He saw a large iron trap chained to the floor. The trap had two great jaws with jagged teeth. The teeth were shiny where they had been sharpened recently.

'You would never escape from a trap like that,' Ratty said. 'The spring on the jaws is so strong.'

'But I must go in there,' Timmy said. 'I have to look for Santa Claus and rescue him.'

'He mightn't be here and what if you get caught in a trap?' Ratty asked.

'It doesn't matter,' Timmy said. 'I have to try.'

'You have no experience in these matters,' Ratty said. 'Mousey and I have lived all our lives avoiding traps and cats. We'll search for you.'

Timmy opened his mouth to protest. But before he could

do so Mousey ran down his trouser leg. He and Ratty slipped through the bars of the grill and into the cellar. Timmy watched them creep across the floor and wriggle through a hole near the door.

There was nothing Timmy could do now but wait. He saw a patch on the floor that was drier than the rest of the tunnel and sat down. He was very tired. His eyelids felt heavy and they began to droop. Again and again he opened them but they continued to droop. Eventually they closed fully and Timmy fell fast asleep. He dreamed he was in a beautiful house. There was a woman there who was kindly looking.

'Look, Timmy,' she said.

Timmy looked and he saw Katie come running across the floor to him.

'I can walk,' Katie said. 'Look, Timmy, I can walk.'

Timmy couldn't speak. He could only stare. Katie could walk again. He couldn't believe it. His dream had come true. He put out his hand to Katie and she took it in hers. But something was wrong. Katie's hand should have been soft and warm. Instead it was cold and rough. It gripped Timmy's hand tightly and hurt. Timmy tried to pull his hand away. But the grip tightened all the more. Timmy cried out in pain and awoke. He opened his eyes and swung his head about and found himself staring into the cruel eyes of Mister Carbuncle.

14
Timmy Escapes Again

Mister Carbuncle laughed and his belly quivered. He still wore Mister Mayor's chain and it jingled and jangled.

'What a good day it has turned out to be after all,' he said. 'I've caught the boy who tried to make a fool of me. Mister Manager has offered a bag of gold for your capture.'

'You'll never get away with it,' Timmy said. 'My friends are helping me. They'll find Santa Claus and release him.'

This made Mister Carbuncle laugh all the more. 'You're an orphan,' he said. 'You have no friends.'

Timmy didn't speak. He didn't want Mister Carbuncle to know that the mice, rats and the birds were his friends. Otherwise there was no knowing what Mister Carbuncle might do.

'I'll tie you up for the night,' Mister Carbuncle said. 'I won't give you anything to eat or drink. Then in the morning

I'll call Mister Manager and tell him to bring me the reward.'

Timmy tried to break free of Mister Carbuncle's grip. But the hand that gripped him through the bars of the grill was like iron.

'Struggle away,' Mister Carbuncle laughed. 'I like boys to struggle.'

'I won't struggle then,' Timmy said.

Mister Carbuncle's face clouded over like the sky on a stormy day. It grew dark. Only his tiny eyes remained bright.

'I'll teach you a lesson in the morning,' he said. 'I'll have you whipped and boiled in oil. Then we'll see you cry and beg for mercy.'

Timmy was frightened but he wasn't going to let Mister Carbuncle know that. 'I won't cry,' he said defiantly. 'And I won't beg either.'

Mister Carbuncle dragged Timmy right up to the grill. 'You'll cry, boy,' he said cruelly. 'And you'll beg too.'

Timmy thought it was wise not to torment Mister Carbuncle any more. So he kept quiet. 'That scared you,' Mister Carbuncle jeered, and he roared for Mister Vicious, who came at a run and stopped in surprise when he saw Timmy.

'Look what I found,' Mister Carbuncle said. 'You're supposed to be on guard. Why is it I have to do everything myself? I'm going to have this boy whipped in the morning and then boiled in oil. I have a good mind to have you

99

whipped as well.'

Mister Vicious cringed in fear. 'I don't like to be whipped,' he said.

'Then get me a rope so that I can tie up this boy,' Mister Carbuncle roared. 'Don't stand there whimpering or I'll have you roasted as well.'

'Yes, sir. Right away, sir.' Mister Vicious rushed around the room in a panic. He couldn't find the door. He ran against the wall and bumped his head. Mister Carbuncle found this very funny and roared with laughter.

Mister Vicious found the door at last and ran out. He soon returned with a length of rope. 'Tie his hands to the bars,' Mister Carbuncle said.

'Aren't you going to bring him inside?' Mister Vicious asked. 'There are rats out there.'

'Of course there are rats out there,' Mister Carbuncle said. 'Why else would I leave the boy outside? The rats won't come inside because of the traps. But they'll come and bite him and nibble off his ears.'

'Oh no, not the rats!' Timmy screamed. 'Please not the rats.' He had to pretend he was frightened of the rats, otherwise the two thugs might become suspicious.

'Who's brave now?' Mister Carbuncle laughed.

'Look at him.' Mister Vicious jeered and chuckled. 'Have you ever seen anyone so frightened in your life?'

But Mister Carbuncle had tired of his game. He struck Mister Vicious. 'Tie him up, you fool,' he growled. 'Do you think I've nothing better to do than to hold him here?'

Timmy made one last effort to escape. But Mister Carbuncle's grip was too strong. Timmy could only watch as Mister Vicious tied his wrists to the bars of the grill.

'We'll leave him now,' Mister Carbuncle said. 'In the morning I will collect a bag of gold for him from Mr Manager.' He rubbed his hands together and he and Mister Vicious left the cellar.

Timmy waited until their footsteps faded. Then he tried to free his hands. But the ropes were tied too tightly. It hurt where they cut into his flesh but he clenched his teeth and didn't cry out. He knew there was little he could do until Mousey and Ratty returned. So he sat down and felt the dampness soak through the seat of his trousers.

The time dragged slowly by. Despite the pain in his wrists Timmy dozed. He awoke to a scuffling noise and saw Mousey scuttling across the floor towards him. Mousey was surprised to see Timmy tied up. Quickly Timmy told him what had happened. 'Did you find Santa Claus?' Timmy asked, forgetting the danger he was in.

Mousey shook his head. 'Ratty and I split up,' he said. 'I took half the house and Ratty took the other half. I searched the rooms and the cupboards and the nooks and crannies. But

Santa Claus isn't here.'

'Maybe Ratty will find him if he's here,' Timmy said. 'In the meantime you must go and get help. I can't escape from these ropes.'

'We have all the help we need right here,' Mousey said. 'A mouse spends most of his life gnawing. My teeth are as sharp as a razor. I will use them to gnaw through the ropes. When Ratty returns he will help me too.'

Mousey began to gnaw. But the ropes were very thick and strong and his small teeth made little progress. From time to time Mousey had to stop to get his breath. He was no longer as young as he used to be. He was glad when Ratty returned, though both he and Timmy were very disappointed to discover Ratty had not found Santa Claus.

Mousey and Ratty set about the task of gnawing through the ropes together. It was a long, difficult task but eventually they cut through the rope binding one of Timmy's wrists. With a hand free, Timmy was now able to undo the knots on the rope himself. Soon he was totally free.

'We must get away from here quickly,' Mousey said. 'But it breaks my heart to leave all the gold and jewels to Mister Carbuncle.'

'And all of it is stolen,' Ratty said. 'It's many the time I've hidden here and watched Mister Carbuncle and his thugs bringing in the gold they'd taken from others, often poor people who would end up going hungry.

'It should be given back to the people it was stolen from,' Mousey said. 'Mister Carbuncle shouldn't be allowed to keep it.'

'Why don't the police take it back?' Timmy asked.

'This is a secret room,' Ratty said. 'The door to it is hidden. Only Mister Carbuncle knows how to get in here.'

'But we know how to get in here now,' Timmy said. 'I could go to the police and tell them.'

Mousey shook his head. 'You can't go to the police,' he said. 'Mister Manager possibly has all the police in the city looking for you.'

'Oh!' Timmy hadn't thought about that. He was glad he had friends like Mousey and Ratty. They knew the ways of the world. But it meant that Mister Carbuncle would get to keep his ill-gotten gains. Unless … Timmy had an idea.

'Why don't we take the gold and jewels?' he said. 'We can hide it and when we find Santa Claus he can tell the police where it is. They can then return it to the people Mister Carbuncle stole it from.'

'Splendid idea!' exclaimed Ratty and Mousey together.

Timmy Goodfellow beamed with pleasure. This was praise indeed from two wise old timers. But then his face fell. How were they to remove the gold and jewels? Even if he filled all his pockets, the large chest would still be filled to the brim.

'Hmm,' Ratty said. 'I've an idea. I'll summon all the rats in the city tonight. They'll help us to carry off the gold and jewels. We'll hide it down here in the tunnels. Mister Carbuncle will never find it.'

'Good thinking, Ratty,' Mousey said. 'We can't have this young fellow here doing all the thinking for us. After all, we're supposed to be wise.'

'Quite so,' Ratty said. 'We have no time to lose. I'll summon help. The signal bell is at the end of this tunnel.'

Ratty went off and after a minute Timmy and Mousey heard the distant peal of a bell. It rang through the tunnels and echoed off the damp walls. Soon they heard the patter of tiny paws. It sounded like thousands of raindrops striking paper. The noise drew near. Soon the tunnel was filled with black rats and grey rats and young rats and old rats and big rats and small rats.

Ratty Rat explained what he wanted them to do. Then the senior rats formed all the others into lines. They all stood to attention. Ratty stared at them for a moment.

'Right then,' he said. 'Let's get to it.'

The rats moved forward in single files. They crawled through the bars of the grill and a number of large rats climbed onto the chests. With their paws, they pushed up the lids of the chests a little way. Other rats then put their heads under the lips of the lids. Slowly they pushed and levered until the lids of the chests were open.

Light was reflected off the gold and jewels. Diamonds sparkled like the stars Timmy had seen earlier in the night. Rubies glowed as red as fire coals. There were emeralds as green as the grass and pearls as white as the petals on the hawthorn. Timmy had never before seen such wealth and he was dazzled by it all.

Now the rats moved forward and climbed onto the chests. Each took a gold piece or a jewel in his mouth. Then they turned smartly and marched away down the tunnel. They were like lines of soldiers and never faltered once. Onward the lines moved seemingly without end. Timmy knew that by morning there wouldn't be a single piece of gold or a solitary jewel left in the cellar. Tomorrow, Mister Carbuncle would be the poorest man in the world.

'Nothing more you can do here,' Ratty said to Timmy and Mousey. 'You had better go back. Perhaps by now the owls will have found Santa Claus. If I can be of help to you, then please come and tell me.'

'Certainly,' Timmy said. 'I'm very grateful to you and your friends. And if ever I can be of help to you, then come and ask me too.'

'Very good,' Ratty said. 'Now, you must be very careful. Remember, when Mister Carbuncle sees his gold and jewels are all gone, he will blame you. He will be angry and will seek revenge.'

'I'll take good care,' Timmy assured him.

'Good,' Ratty said. 'Now, I'll take you back to where you came in. You'll be able to find your way from there.'

Ratty led the way. Timmy followed with Mousey safe in his pocket. When they reached the steps Timmy shook Ratty by the paw.

'Thank you, Ratty,' he said. 'You're a very kind and helpful rat.'

Ratty's whiskers quivered with embarrassment. 'Be off with you now,' he said gruffly. 'It was nothing at all.'

Mousey stuck a paw out of Timmy's pocket and shook Ratty's paw. Without another word, Timmy began to climb the steps. When he'd got through the opening, he looked back. He saw the glow of Ratty's torch below him and raised his hand in farewell. He replaced the grill and slipped through the gap in the hedge. Timmy headed back across the fields to Mrs Haggard's house. On the way his mind was only occupied with thoughts of where Santa Claus might be and how he might find and rescue him.

15
Where is Santa?

It was very late when Timmy reached the house. He crept in and up the stairs. As he passed Mrs Haggard's room he stopped at the door and listened. She was snoring. But Katie was awake and eager to know all that had happened. Timmy recounted the events and she hung her head with sadness when she learned that they hadn't found Santa Claus.

'Don't cry,' Timmy coaxed. 'We'll find him tomorrow. You'll see.'

Mousey excused himself and went off to get some rest. As he had said several times, he was not as young as he once was. Timmy stayed with Katie until she fell asleep. Only then did he go to his own room. He felt sad and disappointed. Even the thought of having taken Mr Carbuncle's gold and jewels didn't cheer him.

Timmy lay on his hard, narrow bed. He was very tired and, despite his sadness, fell asleep. He dreamed of Christmases long past. In his dream his parents were alive and Katie was a baby. They were all together in their warm, safe house. A huge log fire crackled in the grate and the lights on the Christmas tree twinkled. It was snowing and they watched the large flakes tumbling down outside the window.

It was Christmas Eve and Timmy was watching television. The broadcast was coming from the North Pole. Santa Claus was getting ready for his great journey around the world. The reindeer were fed and watered. The sleigh was checked for the last time. Everything was secure. Santa Claus waved to all the watching children and climbed into the sleigh. He shook the reins and shouted out: 'Hup, Hup, Hup.'

Rudolph with the red nose was the lead reindeer. He tossed his head and the bells jingled and the harness jangled. Rudolph cocked his ears and shook his head once more. Then he and the other reindeer strode forward.

They gathered speed as Santa Claus guided them with the reins. Faster and faster they went. Then Santa pulled back on the reins and the reindeer and sleigh lifted up into the sky and flew across the moon. Santa raised a hand and waved and all the elves on the ground cheered and threw their caps into the air.

The television screen went blank and Timmy's mother

sighed. 'Santa Claus is on his way now, Timmy,' she said. 'So you'll have to go to bed.' She put her hand on his shoulder and shook him. In his dream, Timmy smiled at his mother's face above him. But something was wrong. His mother had gripped his shoulder. She shook him violently and it hurt.

Timmy opened his eyes expecting to see his mother's face. But it wasn't his mother who stared down at him. Instead it was an angry face. Spots of red stood out on the pasty cheeks and grey greasy hair hung down like strips of matted fur. It was Mrs Haggard.

'Get up! Get up!' Mrs Haggard screamed. She still shook his shoulder and Timmy realised he had been dreaming all the time. 'Get up, you lazy boy,' Mrs Haggard screamed. 'You never chopped the wood last night. There will be no break-fast for you this morning.'

Timmy's heart sank. He'd been so happy a few moments ago. Now he'd woken to find it was all a dream. His parents were dead. He and Katie were orphans. They would have to live with Mrs Haggard for the rest of their lives. Santa Claus was missing and Timmy didn't know where he was. He'd lost his job at the store and Mister Manager was looking for him. And soon, when Mister Carbuncle found out that all his gold and jewels were missing, he would be seeking Timmy too.

It was with a heavy heart Timmy got up. He said good morning to Katie and went downstairs and out to the yard. It had been frosty and was bitterly cold. The wind blew from the east and it cut through his thin clothing and made him shiver. The axe handle was like a piece of ice. It hurt Timmy's fingers just to grip it.

He began to chop the wood. It was very hard work. The axe was heavy and the wood had been cut from a great beech tree. It was as hard as iron. Timmy sweated. He wished he was still back in his bed and dreaming.

When he'd chopped a great pile of wood he stacked it and replaced the axe in the shed. Then he went back inside.

'No breakfast for you,' Mrs Haggard said. 'You can get up to your room. You're to remain there until I need you.'

Timmy didn't say anything but did as he was told. He climbed the stairs to the attic. He didn't go in to see Katie because he didn't want her to see him sad. In his room he lay on the bed. He was terribly hungry. He hadn't eaten anything since yesterday morning. He hoped he might sleep and dream some more. But he couldn't rest.

Then he heard a tap at the window. He got up, went to the window and saw Beaky Blackbird was outside. Timmy pulled aside the piece of cardboard which covered a broken pane of glass and Beaky hopped into the room.

'Why are you so sad, Timmy?' Beaky asked.

Timmy told him what had happened.

'Well your troubles are over, Timmy – or nearly,' Beaky

said. 'We know where Mister Carbuncle has hidden Santa Claus.'

'Great!' Timmy could hardly contain his excitement. His troubles were forgotten in an instant. 'Tell me,' he said.

'The owls made enquiries last night,' Beaky began. 'They asked everyone they met if they had seen the helicopter. Being wise, they realised that if they could find out where the helicopter had come from then they would find Santa Claus there.'

'Yes, yes,' Timmy said impatiently. 'I see that. But where is Santa Claus? There's no time to lose.'

But Beaky had his story to tell. It was the best story he ever had had to tell. He couldn't bear to cut it short. 'The owls spoke to some cows and a bull. They said they saw Santa Claus arrive in his sleigh. He landed at the old airfield to the west of the city.'

'Yes,' Timmy said. 'And … Come on, Beaky. Get on with your story. I can't wait.'

'I will get on with it when you stop interrupting me,' Beaky insisted. 'Now, where was I? Oh yes. The owls. Now the owls made enquiries …'

'You've already told me that bit,' Timmy cried. 'You were at the airfield on the far side of the city.'

'Was I?' Beaky said. 'I don't remember being out there.'

'Santa Claus was there,' Timmy encouraged, impatiently.

'The cows and the bull said so.'

'Did they tell you as well?' Beaky asked.

'No they didn't,' Timmy said, angrily. 'You just told me.'

'Did I tell you that bit?' Beaky asked. 'I could swear that I hadn't got to that bit yet.'

'You had! You had!' Timmy shouted.

'Well if you say so,' Beaky said, clearly hurt. 'If you don't want to hear the story properly …' He cocked his head to one side and stared at the wall.

'Please, Beaky,' Timmy implored. 'Just tell me where Santa Claus is? You can tell me the whole story later. In fact Katie will want to hear it too.'

'Will she?' Beaky asked. His head went up in the air. 'Oh, it's such a good story.'

'You can tell her now,' Timmy said. 'As soon as you've told me where Santa Claus is hidden.'

'He's hidden in the hanger out at the old airfield,' Beaky said. 'Haven't I already told you that?'

'I must have forgotten,' Timmy said. 'I've also forgotten to tell you you're the most wonderful bird in the whole world.'

'Do you think so?' Beaky asked, vainly. 'Still, I suppose I must be.'

'I have to go,' Timmy said. 'I have to rescue Santa Claus straightaway. Come and tell Katie the story.'

Timmy and Beaky went into Katie's room. 'I know where

Santa Claus is,' Timmy told her. 'I'm going now to rescue him.'

'Be careful, Timmy,' Katie said.

'I will be careful,' Timmy said consolingly. 'While I'm gone Beaky here will tell you the story of how he found out where Santa Claus is hidden. It's a great story, Katie.'

'Oh goody,' Katie said. 'I love stories.'

Timmy was ready to go. At the door he turned to look back. Katie was sitting up in the bed. Beaky was perched on the headboard.

'The owls made enquiries last night, Katie …' Beaky began.

Timmy smiled to himself before he slipped away down the stairs and out of the house. Once outside the smile left his face. He became very serious now. Keeping to the narrow dark streets, he began to make his way to the west of the city where he knew the old airfield was located. There he would find Santa Claus. But how was he to rescue him from the thugs of The Underworld?

16
The Hangar

When Mister Carbuncle woke up he stretched and yawned and scratched under his armpits. The springs of the great bed squeaked and groaned with his movements. Even the floorboards creaked under his vast weight. Slowly Mister Carbuncle opened his eyes. The sun was streaming in the window.

'Oh it's too bright!' he exclaimed, clenching his eyes against the brightness which he detested. He yanked on the bell rope beside his bed and a bell pealed in the distance. In a moment Mister Vicious came running.

'Pull the blinds,' Mister Carbuncle ordered. 'Don't you know how much I hate the sunshine? And bring me my breakfast. I want to have a hearty meal before I whip that boy.'

Mister Vicious brought Mr Carbuncle breakfast. It consisted of six large bowls of strawberry-flavoured ice-cream topped with chocolate sauce. Mister Carbuncle gobbled it all up and rubbed his large belly. He then belched contentedly.

'My clothes,' he ordered and Mister Vicious handed him his trousers, shirt and his two woolly jumpers. Mister Vicious had to put on Mister Carbuncle's shoes and stockings for him, and tie his laces. Mister Carbuncle couldn't bend down because his belly was so big and fat.

'We will go to the cellar now,' Mister Carbuncle declared. 'But first I must get my whip.'

The whip was the whole length of the room. It was as thick as a man's arm at the grip and then tapered down to a fine point hardly thicker than a knitting needle. It was made of the finest plaited leather and cracked like a shot from a rifle. Mister Carbuncle oiled it everyday so the leather was soft and supple. It curled around and around and left red weals on the skin so that anyone who'd been whipped looked like a corkscrew.

Mister Carbuncle lovingly caressed the pliant leather. The whip was his favourite instrument of punishment. He loved to hear it crack and hear the victim's screams. This morning he was going to enjoy himself. He would teach that boy a lesson.

Mister Carbuncle ran down the steps to the cellar. Mister

Vicious followed him, rubbing his hands together. He loved to see small boys being punished.

Mister Carbuncle opened a cupboard door at the foot of the stairs. He pulled a hook hanging inside the cupboard. Suddenly the cupboard began to swing around to reveal a secret panel. Mister Carbuncle now pushed a lever and the secret door to the cellar slid open. Mister Carbuncle stepped into the room where he kept his gold and jewels and stopped in surprise when he saw the two chests with the lids open. He let out a cry of rage and horror and ran to look. They were both empty. His gold and jewels were gone!

He stared into the chests unable to believe his eyes. At first he thought he was having a nightmare. He pinched himself and cried out with the pain. This was no nightmare. This was real. All his gold and jewels had disappeared.

He rushed across the room to where the iron grill was set in the wall. He saw the ends of the rope still tied to the iron bars. But he also saw where the rope had been gnawed through. The boy he'd captured last night was gone. And he had stolen everything!

Mister Carbuncle screamed. He screamed again and again. He lashed out with the whip. It made terrible cracking sounds in the air. With his other hand Mister Carbuncle tore at his hair.

'It's ... it's gone.' Mister Vicious stepped forward and

looked into the empty chests. He had a ridiculous scared look on his face. 'It's all gone,' he repeated. 'And the boy has escaped too.'

Mister Carbuncle swung around. His face was twisted with rage.

'I can see for myself it's all gone,' he roared. 'And the boy has escaped. You … you let him escape. You let him steal all my gold and jewels. Don't stand there. Go and find him and bring him here to me. I'll flay the skin from his back. I'll roast him and toast him and boil him alive.'

Mister Carbuncle cracked the whip. It struck Mister Vicious and curled around his waist. 'Oh! Ah!' Mister Vicious danced on the floor. He spun around to unwind the whip and ran out of the cellar.

Mister Carbuncle kept cracking the whip. 'Ruined,' he muttered, 'I'm ruined. Ruined!' He strode about the room trying to imagine what his gold and jewels looked like. 'I'll get it back,' he muttered. 'I'll make that boy tell me where he's hidden it. When I've got it back I'll pull his teeth out with a pliars. I'll pull his hair out strand by strand. I'll …'

Suddenly Mister Carbuncle sat down in the corner. He rocked backwards and forwards. He wailed. He put his thumb in his mouth and sucked it like a fat baby.

Timmy Goodfellow kept to the shadowy streets as he made his way across the city. He met many poor people on his journey. They were dressed in ragged clothes and looked pinched with the cold. The children too were dressed in ragged clothes and looked hungry. But they all nodded at Timmy and greeted him. From the old clothes he wore and the tired, hungry look in his eye, they knew he was one of them.

'I wish I could help them,' Timmy said to himself. 'But I don't even have enough money to buy food for Katie and myself.'

He soon found himself in the countryside. Here he was no longer afraid of Mister Carbuncle and his thugs or of Mister Manager. They belonged in the city and would never leave it. They wouldn't like the countryside at all.

A farmer came along on a tractor and he gave Timmy a lift.

'You're a long way from the city,' Mister Farmer said. 'You look hungry and cold.'

Timmy admitted that he was and Mister Farmer took him to his home. There Mrs Farmer gave Timmy a large breakfast. There was steaming hot porridge coated with melting honey. Then he ate fresh scrambled eggs on toast. Afterwards he had thick slices of homemade bread spread with butter and washed down with creamy milk.

Timmy ate his fill and, fully satisfied, he thanked Mister and Mrs Farmer and set off on the last part of his journey. He walked two miles before he saw the large aircraft hanger and knew then that he had reached his destination. But he knew too that there were thugs on guard and that he'd have to take great care.

He crawled through a broken gap in the wire fence around the perimeter of the airfield and crept over to a small hut. The hut had no windows, door or roof. But it gave Timmy some shelter. He crouched below the level of the window and looked at the great aircraft hanger. But he still didn't know how he might rescue Santa Claus.

17
Mister Bull Tosses His Head

Timmy Goodfellow looked at the aircraft hanger. All appeared to be quiet. He'd caught a glimpse of one thug who was guarding Santa Claus. But Timmy knew that Mister Carbuncle would have another thug on guard as well. Timmy also knew he could slip into the hanger unnoticed. He knew he could untie Santa Claus' and Rudolph's bonds. But Santa Claus was very old. He wouldn't be able to run. If they tried to escape the thugs would capture them and bring them back. Then Timmy would become a prisoner as well and Santa Claus would never be free.

Timmy regretted not having asked Ratty or Mousey to accompany him. At the very least he could have discussed the matter with them. They were much older and wiser than he. They would have some good ideas as to how he might rescue Santa Claus.

Timmy was tempted to return for them. But he realised he had to act quickly. Mister Carbuncle would have discovered by now that his gold and jewels had been taken away from him. He would know who had done it. He would seek revenge for that. What if he decided to take revenge on Santa Claus? What if he decided to kill Santa?

Timmy shivered at this thought. It made up his mind for him. He had to try and rescue Santa Claus now. But how? Then he remembered that Beaky had told him the owls had spoken to some cows and a bull who were grazing in a field near the airfield. Could he get the bull to help him?

Carefully Timmy crept out of his hiding place and scuttled back to the road. He walked along until he came to the field where the cows were. In a corner, all by himself, stood a great black bull.

Timmy crept round to the corner of the field where the bull stood. 'Psst,' Timmy said.

Mister Bull raised his great head. His large eyes examined Timmy from head to toe. 'Yes boy,' Mister Bull said gruffly. 'Who are you? Why do you disturb me?'

'I'm Timmy Goodfellow,' Timmy said. 'I need your help, sir. You're the only one who can help me. Would you help me, please?'

Mister Bull shifted his weight on his legs. They were as

thick as tree trunks. He swished his tail. His horns were as thick as Timmy's wrists and Timmy couldn't take his eyes off them.

'What is your problem?' Mister Bull asked. 'I never do anything until I know the whole story.'

Quickly Timmy told the story to Mister Bull. He listened intently without saying a word. 'Well, sir?' Timmy eventually asked. 'Will you help me rescue Santa Claus?'

'I have to think about this,' Mister Bull mused. 'It is very foolish to rush headlong into anything without first thinking. You must give me a few minutes to consider all the facts.'

Timmy was impatient. But he kept quiet. He didn't want to upset Mister Bull. He needed him. Without help he would never rescue Santa Claus. Mister Bull seemed to be thinking and thinking. He tossed his head many times. He swished his tail. He shuffled his feet. Then he raised his head and looked Timmy in the eye.

'You're a brave boy, Timmy Goodfellow,' Mister Bull said. 'Santa Claus is lucky to have you as a loyal friend. I will help you. But you must tell me what I'm to do.'

Timmy was overjoyed.

'Come with me,' he said. 'I'll tell you what I want you to do for me.'

Timmy clambered over the fence and walked along the field to the gate. Mister Bull walked beside him. Timmy opened the gate and let Mister Bull out onto the road. Then they walked back to the airfield.

'There are two men guarding Santa Claus,' Timmy explained to Mister Bull. 'I want you to scare them away. When they've run away I'll release Santa Claus and Rudolph. Then we can escape.'

'Very good, Timmy,' Mister Bull said. 'It's been such a long time since I scared anyone. I know I'm going to enjoy this.'

Timmy and Mister Bull crept up to the entrance to the hanger. Mister Bull hung back and Timmy went forward. When he reached the corner of the hanger he called out: 'Santa Claus! Santa Claus! Are you there?'

The two thugs guarding Santa Claus heard Timmy call out. 'It's that boy,' one of them said. 'Let's catch him. Mister Carbuncle will reward us well for his capture.'

The two thugs rushed out of the hanger. Timmy heard them coming. 'You can't catch me!' he cried out.

'There he is,' the thugs shouted. 'Let's get him.'

Timmy ran round the corner of the hanger with the thugs in pursuit. As the thugs turned the corner Mister Bull stepped out from his hiding place and faced them. Mister Bull bellowed. The deafening sound scared even Timmy. Mister Bull shook his head. He pawed at the ground with his hooves. He lowered his head until his sharp, wicked horns were pointing forward.

The thugs seemed stuck to the ground and terror showed on their pasty faces. They gulped and trembled. They tried to speak but their mouths just opened and closed like silent ventriloquists' dummies.

Mister Bull bellowed again. The sound shook the walls of the hanger. Timmy Goodfellow's hair stood on end. The two thugs gave a yelp, turned and ran for their lives. Mister Bull bellowed yet again and then charged after them. The hooves of his great feet pounded the ground, and grass and earth flew up in the air until the sky seemed filled with it.

The thugs split up. One ran this way and the other ran that way. Mister Bull followed one of them. When he caught up to the fleeing thug he butted him in the back with his head. The thug went flying through the air and landed on his face in a muddy puddle.

Mister Bull pushed the man deeper into the puddle with his head. He rolled him around and around until he was wet from head to foot and covered in mud. Only then did Mister Bull leave him and chase the other man. He caught this one's trousers on his horns and whirled him round and round. Then Mister Bull threw the man onto the ground. The thug slowly got to his feet. He appeared to be drunk. He staggered about in a daze and eventually fell down again.

The other thug had got to his feet and was staring around wildly. He saw Mister Bull again and began to run. He was like a muddied scarecrow. Mister Bull took up the chase, caught him and dealt with him in the same way.

Timmy Goodfellow watched and smiled. But he knew he had to act quickly. He didn't know when Mister Carbuncle and his other thugs might arrive. He left Mister Bull to deal with the two thugs and ran around into the hanger.

'Santa!' he called. 'Santa! Where are you?' Timmy stopped and listened. Far away he heard the faint call of Santa Claus.

Timmy rushed towards the sound and could have cried when he saw Santa Claus and Rudolph so cruelly tied up.

'Oh, Santa,' Timmy said, 'am I glad to see you and Rudolph.'

'Are we glad to see you!' Santa smiled gratefully. 'We knew you would come to rescue us. You're a fine boy, Timmy Goodfellow.'

Timmy couldn't help it. He blushed as red as a strawberry.

'I didn't do a lot,' Timmy said modestly. 'I had a lot of help. Now I'd best stop talking and untie you and Rudolph.'

Timmy released the binding on Santa Claus' hands and feet. The old man found it difficult to stand up. His muscles were stiff and sore. Timmy helped him to his feet and offered him his shoulder to lean on until he was able to stand on his own.

'I have an extra suit in the sleigh,' Santa Claus said. 'I'll go and get dressed while you untie Rudolph.' He walked off very slowly and Timmy turned to Rudolph.

'I'm glad you came so quickly, Timmy,' Rudolph whispered. 'Santa Claus is not so young anymore. I was worried about him.'

'He'll be fine now,' Timmy said. 'We'll have the men who imprisoned you arrested and punished and then you can get on with your work. There are a lot of children looking forward to Christmas.'

Quickly Timmy untied Rudolph's bonds. He rubbed the reindeer's legs to increase blood circulation and when Rudolph could walk without limping they went out to where Santa Claus had just finished dressing.

'I'll hitch up the sleigh,' Santa said. 'There's no time to lose.'

'I must go and thank Mister Bull,' Timmy said. 'Without his help I'd never have rescued you.' Timmy went outside. Mister Bull was just walking back towards the hanger.

'Those two thugs won't bother you again, Timmy,' Mister Bull said. 'I taught them a good lesson.'

'Thank you very much, Mister Bull,' Timmy said. 'I would not have been able to rescue Santa Claus without your help.'

'It was a pleasure,' Mister Bull said. 'I haven't had such fun since I was young and used to play with my brothers.'

Just then Santa Claus emerged with Rudolph and the sleigh. 'This is Mister Bull,' Timmy said. 'He helped me rescue you and Rudolph.'

'Thank you, Mister Bull,' Santa Claus said. 'You've done a very good deed today.'

Now it was Mister Bull's turn to blush. 'It was nothing,' he said. 'I just scared those men. And now if you'll excuse me, I must be getting back home.'

They all said goodbye and thanked Mister Bull again. 'Are we ready then, Timmy?' Santa Claus asked. 'Climb up here beside me on the sleigh.'

'Oh!' Timmy could only gulp. He couldn't believe it. He was going to ride in the sleigh. With trembling legs he climbed up beside Santa Claus.

Santa Claus cracked the reins. 'Let's go, Rudolph,' he said.

Rudolph tossed his head and trotted forward. The sleigh bells jingled. When Rudolph had gathered sufficient speed, Santa Claus tugged on the reins. Rudolph lifted his head into the air. A moment later they were airborne. Timmy Goodfellow couldn't believe it. He was actually flying!

18
Timmy Rides in the Mayor's Car

As they flew high above the city, Timmy Goodfellow told Santa Claus all that had happened.

'I lost my job at the store,' Timmy explained. 'Now I don't have enough money to buy food for Katie. And without a job, I can't save enough money for Katie's operation.'

'Don't worry,' Santa Claus said. 'I'll sort all that out for you. Now first of all we must call on Mister Manager.'

'But he'll hand me over to the police,' Timmy said, nervously. 'He has offered a reward for my capture.'

'Don't worry,' Santa Claus said. 'You're my friend. No one is going to hurt you or Katie ever again. Now tell me about the children who came to see me yesterday.'

'I have all the details,' Timmy said. 'I wrote them down in a notebook.' He gave Santa the notebook and told him about

Mrs Needy and her children; and about Mrs Kindheart and how she had no children at all and wanted some of her own.

'It is always sad,' Santa Claus said, 'when a kind woman doesn't have a child of her own. I must see what I can do. It is a pity when a parent can't afford to have presents for their children. But no child will be without a present this Christmas. And that includes you and Katie.'

'Thank you, Santa,' Timmy said, smiling.

They flew over the poor part of the city and Timmy could clearly see the maze of dark narrow streets he had escaped through last night. He told Santa Claus how Teddy Needy had helped him escape and Santa Claus promised to bring a special present to the boy.

Soon they drew near to the city centre. They flew over the Town Hall where Mister Mayor lived and then began to descend. Many children saw the sleigh and waved and cheered. They ran towards Toys Galore and were there when Santa brought Rudolph and the sleigh in to land.

Someone ran into the store and told Mister Manager that Santa Claus had returned. Mister Manager jumped up from his desk and tore at his hair. Santa was here and he didn't have a reception committee waiting for him! He shouted at everyone, rushed outside and then pushed his way through the cheering crowd. He ran up to Santa Claus and stopped in shock when he saw Timmy Goodfellow.

'It's … it's him!' Mister Manager clenched his fists in anger. 'It's … it's that boy! Call the police immediately. I want him arrested.'

Timmy Goodfellow edged closer to Santa Claus. But he need not have worried. Santa Claus held up his hand for silence.

'I did not come here yesterday,' he said. 'The man who came here was an impostor. His name is Mister Carbuncle. He's the boss of The Underworld.'

A great cry went up from the crowd. They had heard of Mister Carbuncle and knew he was a cruel, heartless man.

'I was kidnapped by this Mister Carbuncle,' Santa Claus said. 'But my friend Timmy Goodfellow rescued me. If he hadn't rescued me then we would have had no Christmas. Now I want you all to give three cheers for Timmy.'

The crowd cheered. 'Hip hip hooray! Hip hip hooray! Hip hip hooray!'

Timmy Goodfellow blushed at the acclamation. If only Katie were here to see it. He stared around at all the happy smiling faces and was glad. He had helped to make them all happy. It was a good feeling.

'Now then,' Santa said, 'my good friend Timmy here has taken down all the details you gave the impostor yesterday. So all you children will receive your presents on Christmas morning.'

'Hooray for Timmy!' they shouted. 'Hooray for Timmy!'

Santa Claus waved to the crowd and, with Timmy beside him, strode into Toys Galore. Mister Manager followed.

'I'm so sorry,' he said. 'I …'

But Santa didn't speak. Instead he strode straight to Mister Manager's office.

'There's no time to lose,' Santa Claus said to Mister Manager. 'Call Mister Mayor immediately. Tell him I wish to speak with him urgently. Have Rudolph fed and watered and please bring me some food. I am very hungry.'

'Certainly,' Mister Manager said. 'Whatever you say.' He picked up the telephone on his desk and called Mister Mayor. Then he ordered a meal for Santa Claus.

Mister Mayor soon arrived. Without his chain of office he no longer looked so pompous. Santa Claus told Mister Mayor about Mister Carbuncle and all the thugs in The Underworld.

'That … that evil man,' Mister Mayor spluttered. 'He stole my chain of office. I will have him dealt with.'

'You must have him and all his thugs arrested,' Santa Claus said. 'They must be tried and put in prison. Now our good friend, Timmy Goodfellow, has taken all of Mister Carbuncle's gold and jewels from him. It is hidden down in the old sewers. I want you to bring it to the Town Hall and give it to the poor people of the city. Then they can buy food and clothes and have a good Christmas.'

'It will be done,' Mister Mayor said. 'I will see to it imme-diately.'

'Timmy Goodfellow knows where The Thieves' Den is,' Santa Claus said. 'He will lead the police there. Won't you, Timmy?'

Timmy nodded. He was worried about going into The Thieves' Den but he didn't let his fears show. He couldn't let Santa Claus down.

'Very good then,' Santa Claus said.

When the police arrived Timmy forgot his fear and worry. Soon he was racing through the city in a police car. Behind them six other police cars raced in single file. Their sirens blared and the blue lights winked back at Timmy from the windows of the shops. Timmy sat beside Mister Inspector. He looked grim and determined. Timmy felt the excitement slowly creep up on him. He gazed out as the houses and shops flashed past. People stood on the pavement and stared. A whisper went through the crowds that the brave boy, Timmy Goodfellow, was leading the police to The Thieves' Den.

People waved and called Timmy's name out loud.

'They're cheering you, Timmy,' Mister Inspector said. "You're more popular than Mister Mayor. If you were to stand against Mister Mayor in the next election I think you would win.'

Timmy directed the driver to The Thieves' Den. The

police cars roared into the street and stopped with a screech of brakes. Doors opened and the policemen burst out of the cars. Immediately they surrounded the great, evil house.

Mister Inspector led his men up to the front door. They didn't bother to knock but two burly policemen placed their shoulders to the door and broke it down. The police then burst into the building with Timmy on their heels.

They rushed through and captured the thugs. Mister Vicious was caught hiding in a wardrobe. Mister Illegal was found in the study. He began to read out his rights under the law. But two policemen placed handcuffs on his wrists and led him away.

There was no sign of Mister Carbuncle. He had escaped. Timmy Goodfellow remembered the cellar and the tunnels. Were the tunnels Mister Carbuncle's means of escape? Without thinking of the danger, Timmy dashed down to the cellar. He found the secret door was open and went through to Mister Carbuncle's secret room. Here he noticed that the iron grill to which he had been tied was thrown in the corner. Mister Carbuncle had clearly made his escape that way.

Timmy didn't hesitate. He slipped through the opening down into the dark tunnel. Immediately he felt the damp and chill. But he clenched his teeth and began to run forward. As his eyes became accustomed to the gloom, he ran faster and faster.

He remembered the tunnels from the night before. So as fast as his legs would carry him he ran towards where the bell which summoned the rats hung. When he reached it he tugged the chain vigorously. The bell rang out through the great tunnels. It was a lonesome, eerie sound. Again and again Timmy tugged the chain. Soon the echoes merged with the peal of the bell until there was a continuous ringing sound.

Timmy stopped and listened. Soon he heard the patter of many paws. Rats converged on the ringing bell from all directions. They gathered in a great crowd and stared in amazement at Timmy. Ratty Rat soon arrived, puffing and out of breath.

'What's this all about?' he demanded. 'Something serious must be up if the bell is rung.'

'It's me, Ratty,' Timmy said. 'I rang the bell. Mister Carbuncle has escaped down into these tunnels. I have to find him and I need your help.'

'Certainly we will help you, Timmy,' Ratty said. 'So there's no time to lose. All you rats spread out. Search all the tunnels. When you find Mister Carbuncle drive him back towards us. Quickly now.' Ratty clapped his paws together and the rats turned and raced back down the tunnels.

'We'll wait here,' Ratty said. 'I have every confidence that my rats will find your quarry and bring him back here to us.

Now then, Timmy, tell me what's been happening? Did you find Santa Claus?'

Timmy recounted his exciting story for Ratty. 'What an adventure to have,' Ratty said, highly impressed. 'It reminds me of the sort of adventures I had when I was your age. How I sometimes wish I was a young rat again.' Ratty sighed, thinking of his exciting youth.

'But if you were young,' Timmy said, 'then we wouldn't have a wise old rat at all. A young rat can run and chase. But only a wise rat can think.'

'That's absolutely right, of course,' Ratty said with satisfaction. 'You're a wise boy, Timmy Goodfellow. No wonder Santa Claus asked you to help him.'

Timmy blushed again. What a day it had been for praise and adventure! He would have a great story for Katie. The mice and the birds would have to hear it too. After all, without their help he wouldn't have succeeded.

Ratty pricked up his ears. He cocked his head to one side so that he could hear much better. 'They've caught him,' he said with much delight. 'I can hear them. They're coming this way.'

Timmy could hear nothing. But as he listened more closely he heard a great hubbub in the distance. Slowly the noise came closer. Then Timmy glimpsed a large group of rats coming towards him. In their midst was Mister Carbuncle.

His face was pale and he looked terrified. His eyes stared wildly about him. He hated rats. It was why he had the traps set in The Thieves' Den. Now, when he saw Timmy, his face became hopeful.

'Help me,' he pleaded. 'Please help me. Make those rats go away. They're horrible creatures. Horrible. I'll give you anything you want. How much gold and jewels do you want?'

'You have no gold and jewels any more,' Timmy said.

'I'll give you my chain,' Mister Carbuncle said. 'It's pure gold. You can have it.' Mister Carbuncle took off the chain which had belonged to Mister Mayor and handed it to Timmy. 'I'll get more gold for you,' he said. 'I'll rob banks. You can be the new boss of The Underworld. Only help me.'

'Come with me then,' Timmy said. 'And you'll be safe.'

'Anything! Anything!' Mister Carbuncle stared around him. But when he saw all the rats staring at him, he screwed his eyes shut and shook like a tree in the wind.

'This way,' Timmy said. He took Mister Carbuncle's arm and led him forward. 'Thanks again, Ratty,' Timmy said. 'When this is all over I will come and visit you.'

'I look forward to that, Timmy,' Ratty said.

Timmy said goodbye to Ratty and his friends and began to lead Mister Carbuncle down the tunnel towards The Thieves' Den. 'Don't open your eyes,' he said. 'Otherwise the rats will return.'

'I won't,' Mister Carbuncle said fervently. 'I hate those creatures.'

Timmy led Mister Carbuncle back to the cellar. There he found Mister Inspector and a number of the policemen. Immediately the policemen took Mister Carbuncle by the arms and placed handcuffs on his wrists. Mr Carbuncle was shocked.

'I've been betrayed,' Mister Carbuncle wailed. 'That boy has double crossed me. I'll get him for this. Look, he's stolen Mister Mayor's chain. Arrest him. He's a thief!'

'Be quiet,' Mister Inspector ordered. His voice was stern. Mister Carbuncle shut up. 'Take him away to jail,' Mister Inspector said. 'Put him in our strongest cell.'

Kicking and crying, Mister Carbuncle was dragged away to jail.

'You've done a wonderful job, Timmy,' Mister Inspector said. 'We've caught all of Mister Carbuncle's gang. Now they will go to prison for a great many years and people will no longer live in fear. It's all thanks to you.'

He took Timmy back upstairs. Mister Mayor had arrived at The Thieves' Den and he shook Timmy's hand and took back his chain of office.

'You've done a fantastic job, Timmy,' Mister Mayor said. 'As a reward I'm going to confer on you the freedom of the city. You can have anything you want. Now, we must return to Toys Galore.'

Timmy could hardly believe it all. He walked out of The Thieves' Den in a daze. When he reached the front door there was a large group of people waiting outside. They had notebooks and pens and tape recorders. Flashbulbs went off and television cameras began to roll. They were asking questions of Timmy all at once.

'You're famous now, Timmy,' Mister Mayor said. 'These reporters are from every country in the world. Today you will be on television all over the globe. And your picture will be on the front page of every newspaper too.'

Timmy blushed yet again. He felt like a Hollywood film star or a famous footballer. He told the reporters the whole story and how the animals and the birds had helped him. The reporters recorded every word.

'Thank you, Timmy,' they said when it was all over. 'You've saved Christmas and caught the most terrible gang of crooks in the whole world.'

'That's all now. That's all now. Thank you ladies and gentlemen,' Mister Mayor interrupted them. Now that he had his chain of office back, he was almost his old self again. 'We must return to Toys Galore. Santa Claus is waiting for us. We must not delay.'

Mister Mayor ushered Timmy ahead of him out to the street. Waiting at the edge of the pavement was Mister

Mayor's official black car. It was as long as two cars placed end to end. A uniformed chauffeur opened the door for Timmy and Mister Mayor. They got in.

The car was luxurious. Timmy smelled the real leather seats. They were soft and comfortable. He sank back into them and yawned. He was very tired but he wasn't going to sleep. Today was the most exciting day of his life and he was going to enjoy every minute of it.

There was a television in the car and Mister Mayor switched it on. Timmy couldn't believe his eyes. There he was on the screen, talking to the reporters. What would Katie think of him? Or Mrs Haggard? The thought of Mrs Haggard dampened Timmy's enthusiasm a little. When this was all over he would have to return to that house. He and Katie would have to continue living there. They would be hungry and cold and lonesome again.

But maybe Santa Claus could persuade Mister Manager to give him his job back at the store. That way he would have some extra money again. He could keep on saving and Katie would eventually have her operation.

Timmy cheered up again. Santa Claus would help him. He looked at the screen once more. The scene changed to the Town Hall. Here there was a great crowd gathered at the entrance. Timmy could tell from the way people were dressed that they were poor.

In the crowd he saw Mrs Needy. Her children, including Teddy, were with her. Timmy watched them go up the steps of the Town Hall. On the top step an official stood behind a large table. It was piled high with gold and jewels. As the people went forward each was given a fistful of gold and jewels.

'No one will be hungry or cold this Christmas,' Mister Mayor said. 'As you can see we are handing out Mister Carbuncle's gold and jewels.'

Mrs Needy received her share and came back down the steps. A reporter stepped forward and held out a microphone.

'I'm so happy,' Mrs Needy said. 'We won't go hungry or feel cold this Christmas. It's thanks to that wonderful boy, Timmy Goodfellow. I want to thank him. He has done a great job for all the people in the city and for all the children in the whole world.'

'Everyone is singing your praises, Timmy,' Mister Mayor said. 'They all love you very much.'

Timmy couldn't speak. There was a lump in his throat. So he remained silent as they completed the journey to Toys Galore. Here, a great crowd was gathered outside the store. When they saw Timmy in Mister Mayor's car they cheered and waved. Timmy waved back. He felt like a prince. When the car stopped before the entrance to the store Mister Manager ran forward and opened the door. He led Timmy and Mister Mayor into the store and along to the office where Santa Claus was waiting for them.

19

Mrs Haggard Opens an Envelope

Mrs Haggard ate her breakfast. She had a large bowl of porridge and then ate three boiled eggs. She had tea and toast with marmalade. Then she sat down to watch her favourite quiz programme on the television. Suddenly the screen went blank. A man appeared after a few moments.

'We are interrupting this programme with a newsflash,' the man said. 'We are now going over to Mister Reporter.'

The picture changed to a house in the city.

'Behind me,' Mister Reporter said, 'is the Thieves' Den. This morning a young boy from this city named Timmy Goodfellow led the police here. All the thugs of The Underworld and their boss, Mister Carbuncle, were arrested.'

Mrs Haggard sat bolt upright in her chair. They couldn't possibly be referring to the Timmy Goodfellow she knew. He was lazy and would sneak off at every opportunity. He hadn't even chopped the wood last night. Obviously there was another Timmy Goodfellow in the city.

'Timmy Goodfellow himself captured Mister Carbuncle,' Mister Reporter continued. 'Mister Inspector said that it was the bravest thing he has ever seen. After all, Mister Carbuncle is the most feared man in the world. Also last night Timmy Goodfellow removed Mister Carbuncle's gold and jewels. He hid them in the old city sewers and now they are all being handed out to the poor of the city.'

'On no!' Mrs Haggard moaned. 'I won't get any of it at all. If only I dressed up as a poor person, perhaps they would give me a selection of the gold and jewels.'

'Something is happening,' Mister Reporter said excitedly. 'I think Timmy Goodfellow is coming out of The Thieves' Den. There is a great crush about me here. Everyone wants to see and speak with this hero.'

The picture shook on the television screen. Then it steadied again. The door of The Thieves' Den appeared. It opened and Mister Mayor and Mister Inspector came out. Between them walked Timmy Goodfellow.

'It's … it's him!' Mrs Haggard spluttered in disbelief. 'It's that lazy good-for-nothing boy.' The words stuck in her throat like fish bones. She could only watch with her mouth hanging open as Timmy told his story. 'I'll flog him,' Mrs Haggard screamed. 'I'll give him no food for a month. I'll tear his hair out from the roots.'

She watched as Timmy finished his story and went out to Mister Mayor's car. The camera followed the car until it disappeared at the corner of the street.

'It's been announced,' Mister Reporter continued, 'that Mister Mayor has conferred on Timmy Goodfellow the freedom of the city. Timmy can now have anything he wants. And of course Timmy will receive a large reward for the capture of Mister Carbuncle and his gang.'

At this Mrs Haggard rubbed her hands together. Timmy could have anything he wanted as well as a large reward. Well he wouldn't be allowed to keep it. She would take it for herself. After all, she looked after him. It was only right that she should have it all.

'Now,' Mister Reporter said, 'we're going over to the Town Hall.' The picture on the screen changed. Mrs Haggard watched as the poor people of the city gathered at the Town Hall. Her eyes greedily watched the piles of gold and jewels on the table. 'I'll punish that boy,' she said. 'He should have brought all that gold and jewels back here to me. After all, I take such good care of himself and his ungrateful sister.'

The screen changed again. Now Mrs Haggard saw the entrance to Toys Galore. She saw the great, cheering crowd. She saw Mister Mayor's great car drive up to the entrance.

143

She saw Mister Manager open the door and Timmy Goodfellow and Mister Mayor emerge. She saw Timmy and Mister Mayor wave to the crowd and then go into the store.

'Flogged,' Mrs Haggard said between clenched teeth. 'I'll have him flayed until the flesh falls from his body.' She couldn't bear to see any more, switched off the television and sat back in the chair. She bit her nails viciously.

Suddenly a cruel idea formed in her mind. She knew Timmy loved his sister very much. Well, she would get rid of Katie. She wasn't able to work and she cost as much as Timmy to feed.

'I'll throw her out of the house,' Mrs Haggard said to herself gloatingly. 'It is bitterly cold outside and she will get frostbite. That will teach that ungrateful boy a lesson.'

Pleased with her plan, Mrs Haggard jumped to her feet. She rushed upstairs to Katie's room.

'I'm going to throw you out of my house,' Mrs Haggard announced. She bustled about the room, gathered together Katie's clothes and wrapped them in a bundle.

'Please don't throw me out, Mrs Haggard,' Katie pleaded. 'It's so cold and I don't have anywhere to go. Timmy is the only person I have in the whole world. He would be heartbroken without me.'

'Don't I know,' Mrs Haggard jeered. She laughed in her cruel, callous way and Katie clasped her little hands together and began to cry.

Santa Claus was delighted to see Timmy back safe. 'I've heard of all the good things you've done,' Santa Claus said. 'So now it is our turn to do something for you. Mister Mayor will now take you in his car. Are you ready, Mister Mayor?'

'I'm ready, Santa Claus,' Mister Mayor said.

Santa Claus picked up an envelope from the desk and handed it to Mister Mayor who led the way out to his car. Soon Timmy was again racing though the city. Now he recognised where he was. They were heading towards Mrs Haggard's house.

Timmy could hardly wait to tell Katie all that had happened. She would be so thrilled and excited. Mrs Haggard, would be angry though. She would punish him for what he'd done. But he could accept that if Katie was happy.

The large, black limousine drove into the street where Timmy lived and stopped before Mrs Haggard's house. Timmy and Mister Mayor got out of the car. They walked up to the door and rang the bell.

Mrs Haggard was dragging Katie from her bed when she heard the bell ring. Leaving the little girl for the moment, she went downstairs and answered the door. When she saw Mister Mayor with Timmy she opened her mouth in surprise.

'Oh,' she said. 'I suppose you've come with the reward.' She stared at the envelope in Mister Mayor's hand.

'It's not a reward,' Mister Mayor said. 'It's a gift for Timmy and his sister Katie from Santa Claus.'

'I'm their guardian,' Mrs Haggard said. 'I should have it. After all, they cost me a fortune to feed and clothe. And that boy is so lazy and ungrateful.'

'Maybe you shouldn't have it,' Mister Mayor said.

'Give it to me,' Mrs Haggard said. 'I demand that you give it to me.'

'You heard that, Timmy,' Mister Mayor said. 'Mrs Haggard has agreed to accept this envelope.'

'That is correct, Mister Mayor,' Timmy said.

'Now you must assure me,' Mister Mayor said to Mrs Haggard, 'that you will agree to do what is asked of you.'

'Oh I agree,' Mrs Haggard said. 'I agree to everything. Now give it to me.' She snatched the envelope from Mister Mayor and tore it open. But it contained only a single sheet of paper with an official stamp on it. 'What's this?' Mrs Haggard asked. 'There is no money in this envelope. Are you trying to deceive me? I know my rights.'

'I'm glad to hear that,' Mister Mayor said. 'Now if you look at that sheet of paper you will soon realise that it is a legal document. It was signed this morning by Mister Legal.'

'What's it about?' Mrs Haggard demanded.

'Mister Legal orders you to hand over Timmy and Katie Goodfellow to me,' Mister Mayor said. 'I will then take them both to another home where they will be looked after properly. The woman there will love them and not treat them cruelly.'

Timmy could hardly believe his ears. He and Katie were to escape at last from Mrs Haggard's clutches. They would be free!

'Never!' Mrs Haggard screamed. 'They will never leave here. They are both ungrateful children. I won't allow it. I won't agree. If they go they can't take the money. I was told I could keep it. I was made a promise ...'

'You are a wicked, evil woman,' Mister Mayor said. 'You have treated these two children in a terrible manner. You have made them go hungry and cold. You wouldn't pay for Katie's operation. Now you are going to lose them. Stand out of our way.'

Mister Mayor strode into the house. Mrs Haggard stood to one side. She was beaten. Timmy too entered the house and led Mister Mayor upstairs to the attic where Katie was.

'Oh I'm so glad you've come, Timmy,' Katie said gratefully, and with tears in her eyes. 'That horrible Mrs Haggard was about to throw me out of the house. I was so frightened.'

'There's no need to be frightened any more,' Timmy said. 'You're safe now. And look who's come to visit you.'

Katie's eyes opened wide in surprise. She couldn't believe

it. She was unable to speak. Mister Mayor shook hands with her. 'We've come to take you away, Katie,' he said.

'Take me away?' Katie was puzzled.

'We're leaving Mrs Haggard,' Timmy said. 'We're going to a new home where you'll be looked after. We won't ever be hungry or cold again.'

'Oh Timmy,' Katie said joyfully. 'I can hardly believe it.'

'We'd best get going,' Mister Mayor said. 'There's a kind lady waiting for you both.'

Timmy packed his few belongings. Mister Mayor then called his driver from the car and he carried Katie out of Mrs Haggard's house forever.

Timmy called Mousey to say goodbye and they promised to visit each other. Then Timmy summoned the birds. Beaky and Robby and Chirpy and Chalky came to see them off. 'We'll come and see you, Timmy,' they all said.

Timmy walked down the stairs for the last time. Mrs Haggard stood in the hall. She held the sheet of paper in her hands and was staring at it speechless. Timmy walked out of the house and got into Mister Mayor's car beside Katie. As they drove away, neither Katie nor Timmy looked back.

20
The Happiest Christmas of All

On the journey Timmy told Katie about his adventures. 'There is a large reward offered for the capture of Mister Carbuncle and his thugs,' Timmy said. 'Now I'm going to be able to pay for your operation. Soon you'll be able to walk again.'

'I can hardly believe it,' Katie said. 'From now on everything will be fine. Santa Claus is so kind. I wish I could have met him.'

'He's very busy,' Timmy said. 'But maybe he'll see you next year.'

'That'll be lovely,' Katie said. She sat back into the warm leather seat. It felt so comfortable. She hadn't felt so warm in ages.

The car sped through the city. People recognised Mister

Mayor's crest on the bonnet. They recognised Timmy Good-fellow too. They waved and cheered as the car passed.

'Wave to the people, Katie,' Timmy said.

'Oh I couldn't,' Katie said, shyly.

'They want you to wave,' Timmy said. 'It will make them happy.'

'Oh I'll wave then,' Katie said. She raised her hand and waved to the passing crowd. She waved until her hand ached. She was happy. All those people were happy for her too. It was the best day of her life so far.

The great car with Mister Mayor's crest on the bonnet reached the outskirts of the city. Here there were long straight roads with large houses on each side. Gigantic oak trees grew along the pavements. They were bare and blackened in the winter sunshine.

The car turned into another road. It was narrower than any road Timmy had ever seen. Halfway down, the car turned in through a gateway. Before them, at the end of a tree-lined driveway, stood a cottage.

It wasn't an ordinary cottage though. It was like a cottage from a fairy tale. The roof was thatched and had two dormer windows. The whitewashed walls were all crooked and the chimneys were twisted. The door was very low and had black hinges and a knocker. The leaded windows were tiny and the glass sparkled in the sunshine. All around the door were climbing rose bushes, though of course there were no flowers to be seen since it was winter.

Mister Mayor's car stopped before the cottage door.

'Here we are,' he said. 'This is your new home.'

'Oh!' Timmy and Katie chorused. They both stared in wonder at the cottage.

'It's a wonderful cottage,' Mister Mayor said. 'It's very old and it has secret passageways and rooms. It's the best place I know of for playing hide and seek and blindman's buff. I know you'll both be very happy here.'

'I know we will too,' Timmy agreed smiling happily.

'Let's go in then,' Mister Mayor said. He and Timmy got out of the car and Mister Mayor's driver picked Katie up in his arms and carried her. Mister Mayor knocked at the front door.

The door opened and Timmy gasped in surprise. Standing in the doorway was Mrs Kindheart, the lady who'd come to see Santa Claus the day before.

'You're all very welcome to Friendly Cottage,' Mrs Kindheart said. She shook hands with Mister Mayor and Timmy, and bent down to kiss Katie's cheek. 'This is now your new home,' Mrs Kindheart said. 'I hope you will be very happy here. I love children but I do not have any of my own. From now on you will be my children. Do you agree?'

'Oh yes!' Timmy and Katie said together.

They entered a narrow hall. It was lined in real oak and

there were great beams across the ceiling. The floor was flagged. On the wall hung a number of paintings and at the end of the hall a grandfather clock ticked importantly.

'This way,' Mrs Kindheart called and she led them into a large sitting-room. It also had beams in the ceiling. There were comfortable armchairs and a nest of tables. Before the great log fire burning in the fireplace a black cat lay asleep on a rug. 'This is Mister Tom,' Mrs Kindheart said. 'You will meet him later when he wakes up. And this is for you, Katie.' Mrs Kindheart indicated a wheelchair in a corner of the room. 'It works by battery. You will be able to get around easily in it until you have your operation.'

'Thank you,' Katie said gratefully. 'Can I try it out?'

'You certainly can,' Mrs Kindheart laughed.

The driver sat Katie in the chair. Mrs Kindheart showed Katie how to operate the controls. Soon she was speeding about the floor, laughing gaily. Timmy thought he had never seen her so happy since before the accident.

'Now I will show you your rooms,' Mrs Kindheart said. She led the way upstairs and Timmy followed. Mister Mayor's driver carried Katie. The rooms were in the attic, with the two dormer windows. But they were not like the rooms in Mrs Haggard's house.

Here the ceilings were low and the roof beams exposed. There were no gaps in the thatched roof and the rooms were warm and snug. In each was a bed with a feather mattress that was soft and comfortable. There was a quilt on each bed filled with duck down that made it as cosy as an animal's nest. There were wardrobes too, filled with all the clothes and shoes Katie and Timmy might ever wish to have.

Next to the bedrooms was another room with a dormer window facing out onto the rear garden. Here there were chests filled with toys. There was a railway track running over the floor with signals and sidings and stations – and three trains. There was a fine wooden rocking horse. There were dolls and prams and a doll's house crammed with miniature furniture.

'We'll be happy here,' Timmy said. There were tears in his eyes but he was determined that he wouldn't cry. After all, he was Timmy Goodfellow, the boy who'd captured the most feared criminal in the whole world.

'Now,' Mrs Kindheart said, 'we have one more surprise for you.' She led them downstairs to the hall. 'Wait here,' she said. She walked into the sitting-room. After a moment she called for them to come and they all joined her. Standing in the centre of the room was Santa Claus.

'Oh!' It was all Katie could say. Her eyes opened wide in surprise. She stared at Santa Claus and tried to speak. But no sound came from her mouth.

'Hello, Katie,' Santa Claus said, warmly. 'We meet at last.'

He walked forward and took Katie's hand, which trembled with excitement.

'Hel … Hello, San … Santa,' Katie managed to say.

Santa Claus laughed. He quivered like a jelly. Timmy and Mrs Kindheart and Mister Mayor laughed too. Then Katie laughed. They laughed and laughed until tears streamed down their cheeks. Their laughter woke Mister Tom and he raised his head and stared at them.

'I'm trying to have a catnap,' Mister Tom said. 'Would you mind not making so much noise?'

'Sorry, Mister Tom,' Mrs Kindheart said. 'We didn't mean to wake you.'

They stood around while they got their breath back.

'Now,' Santa said, 'I'm a very busy man. I've lots of children to see before Christmas Eve. On Christmas Eve I've got a very busy night too. So I'll have to be off. But I know I will not have any problems because my good friend Timmy Goodfellow here is going to come with me and operate my computer.'

'Really!' Timmy gasped, unable to say another word.

'Are you ready, Timmy?' Santa Claus asked.

Timmy could only nod his head.

'Good,' Santa Claus said. 'But we're not forgetting Katie. We have a very special treat for you too.'

Katie's eyes opened wide in surprise. Santa Claus smiled at her.

'Just for you, Katie,' he said. 'Because you've been such a brave girl. Now let's go. We have much to do.'

Santa Claus led the way outside. Before the door stood Rudolph and the sleigh. Santa Claus introduced Katie to Rudolph.

'Pleased to meet you, Katie,' Rudolph said.

'And I'm delighted to meet you,' Katie said. 'I know that you are a very famous reindeer. I heard a song on the radio about you.'

Rudolph blushed. 'Oh yes,' he said. 'That song ...'

'All aboard,' Santa Claus said. 'All aboard.' He climbed up onto the sleigh and Timmy climbed up beside him. 'Now you, Katie,' Santa Claus said.

'Me?' Katie stared in surprise.

'It's your treat,' Santa said. 'You're coming for a ride in the sleigh.'

Katie was speechless as Mister Mayor's driver lifted her up beside Timmy and Santa Claus.

'Goodbye for now, Katie and Timmy,' Mrs Kindheart called to them.

'Goodbye, Mrs Kindheart,' they both echoed. 'We'll see you later.'

'Ready?' Santa Claus asked. 'Then let's go.' He picked up the reins and shook them. Rudolph moved forward. He raced down the driveway to the gate. But before they reached the gate Santa Claus tugged back on the reins. Rudolph lifted his head into the air and a moment later they flew over the gate and climbed faster and faster up into the sky.

Santa Claus brought Rudolph around in a great circle. In a moment they were flying over the cottage. Below, Mrs Kindheart seemed very small. She was waving and Timmy and Katie waved back. They could see Mister Mayor's car heading towards the gate. It was hardly bigger than a toy motorcar.

'Ho,ho,ho!' Santa Claus called out.

Rudolph tossed his great head. His feet beat the air faster and faster. They gathered speed. Katie clung onto Timmy as they sped across the sky. It was, she thought, the happiest day of their whole lives.

The End